"Richard Wenzel has done it again. In *Dreams of Troy*, his characters M15 agent Elizabeth Foster and American infectious diseases expert Jake Evans face another ingenious international terrorist plot. Who knew that computer malware introduced into the world's medical systems could topple governments? Dr. Wenzel did, and his well-crafted thriller—this time unfolding in Spain with implications across the Mediterranean—keeps you riveted at every plot twist."

    —Dean King, author of *Skeletons on the Zahara* and *The Feud*

"Beyond the current headlines of ransom ware disabling hospital systems, deeper threats exist that have the potential to disable, hijack or interrupt critical medical delivery systems. In *Dreams of Troy*, Richard Wenzel probes into the real cyber attack surface of medicine while weaving an exciting and engaging page turner."

    – Eric Perakslis

    Healthcare Cyber Security Expert. Senior Vice President and Head, Takeda Data Science Institute. Visiting Faculty, Department of Biomedical Informatics, Harvard Medical School.

"An internationally acclaimed infectious diseases expert and epidemiologist, Richard Wenzel uses his extensive insights to portray a chilling story of cyber terrorism in his book *Dreams of Troy*. Thought-provoking and engaging, the plot unfolds in a most understandable yet unpredictable manner. A page-turning thriller, it is packed full of puzzling twists and turns."

    – Kathryn Kahler Vose

    Former President, The National Press Club, Washington, DC

"Be prepared to stay up all night reading *Dreams of Troy*, Richard Wenzel's gripping medical thriller and tale of international suspense. In our age of big data, biomedical engineering, and cyber security breaches, his premise is chillingly realistic, his pace never slacking as he lures us into a turbulent world of characters motivated by romance, vengeance, greed, self-protection, and service to country. A thoroughly entertaining, well-crafted, and informative read in an evocative international setting."

    – Helen Montague Prichard Foster, Author of *Emily and Henry*

# DREAMS OF TROY

6 December 2017
White Stone, VA

To Anne Picillo

W.R best wishes to a
fellow Author - Just received
your new book! Let us know
if you come to Virginia

Dick Wen,

# DREAMS OF TROY

RICHARD P. WENZEL

ISBN-13: 978-1975920944

This work is fictional, and any resemblance to people living is coincidental.

Also by Richard P. Wenzel
*Stalking Microbes*
*Labyrinth of Terror*

Author photo by Jeff Cherry

Book design by Wendy Daniel

Editorial review by Joni Albrecht

# DEDICATION

To my brother Al and sisters Betsy and Suzy, who shared
the beginning, life's first poetry.

# ACKNOWLEDGMENTS

Special thanks to Joni Albrecht, an extraordinary editor who kept me focused on improving the story while inspiring creativity. Thanks to Kenny Marotta for initial editorial review and to my wife, JoGail, for offering critiques of several versions of the book. Author Helen Foster has been a valuable critic of my manuscript. I am grateful to Barbara Briley, longtime friend and assistant, who formatted various drafts along the way. I also thank Connie Brothers at the Iowa Writer's Workshop for the continual encouragement and Ellen Trumposky for the excellent copy editing prior to publication.

*Scarring his own body with mortifying strokes, throwing filthy rags*
*on his back like any slave, he slipped into the enemy's city,*
*roamed its streets – all disguised, a totally different man,*
*a beggar, hardly the figure he cut among Achaea's ships.*
*That's how Odysseus infiltrated Troy, and no one knew him at all…*

The Odyssey by Homer
Book 4:274 – 280

*After many years have slipped away, the leaders of the Greeks, opposed by the Fates, and damaged by war built a horse of mountainous size, through Pallas's divine art, and weave planks of fur over its ribs: they pretend it's a votive offering: this rumor spreads. They secretly hide a picked body of men, chosen by lot, there, in the dark body, filling the belly and the huge cavernous insides with armed warriors.*

The *Aeneid* by Virgil
Book 2: 1-56

*Beware of Greeks Bearing Gifts – Laocoön*

*The Aeneid* by Virgil

Book 2:49

MAP

# PROLOGUE

"**W**e are not only willing warriors," said Amer. "We're committed philosophers prepared to swallow the hemlock if need be." He realized that few might recall what the two did in life, but many sons and daughters would remember how we died.

Neither man would be mistaken for carefree vacationers. Both were in their mid-30s, handsome with thin builds and a mysterious sense of enterprise etched in the lines of their faces. They remained silent for several seconds.

"I narrowly survived, Panos. So many brothers killed. Our PLO itself may be dying. Truly a Black September."

Volleys of giggling that countered the gravity of the men's exchange floated through the air, emanating from the leeward side of a thicket of tamarisk trees that poked through the white sand. Amer had chosen the Aegean Island's beach for a fathers' weekend holiday with his dear friend Panos and Panos's daughter, Kleïs, and his own twin girls, Diana and Sasha. The triple sounds of joy pleased Amer and offered him the space to discuss concerns for the Middle East with Panos over cigarettes, olives, feta cheese, and a traditional drink.

"Look, Sasha," shouted Diana. "The bark is so purple and the flowers are bright pink! So pretty." Sasha, romping in the sand, beamed in full agreement with her 4-year old sister.

Amer applauded each time he heard the girls discuss nature – a gesture which seemed to delight Diana, who immediately scanned the seaside for the next beach treasure. Kleïs focused on counting out loud the number of blossoms on each sapling.

Amer raised his shot glass, looked toward the girls and back to Panos. "To the future, the force that will soon change the world into a better place." Panos joined him with an unfurled arm and a consenting nod. Both men drained the glass in one gulp. Amer immediately poured them each another.

The children ran up close, and Diana asked Kleïs if she had smelled their fathers' drinks. "Smells like licorice. Awful!" Amer chuckled.
Kleïs took in a deep breath, waved away the cigarette smoke, then shrugged her shoulders. "My dad drinks that all the time."

In matching dark blue swim suits, the young trio set to work fashioning sand castles, supporting their structures with seashell fragments and small sticks, decorating some with pieces of indigo-colored bark and stringy bits of seaweed that washed upon the shore. Amer savored the moment, drawn in by each girl's attention to detail and ingenuity.

Diana suggested building a wall around the castle town, which would protect the good people inside from "invaders." Amer knew she had learned the term from his mother-in-law's countless stories of her forced departure from Palestine. Dark memories overshadowed this moment in the sun. There was no escaping his reality.

Sasha kissed her sister's cheek, smiling, "Oh, that's perfect."

As the winds eased, Panos raised his hands in a histrionic gesture and exclaimed skyward, "Thank you, warm Zephyr, for chasing away cool Boreas." All three girls giggled at Panos' appeal to the gods. He removed his sandals, rolled up the cuffs of his tan trousers, grabbed his camera and suggested a walk by the water's edge. The children leaped up from their castles and raced ahead.

With the girls skipping by the surf, Panos turned to Amer, his foolish expression now replaced with a serious stare. "I'm so happy you can take a break like this, Amer. You deserve it."

"The refugee camps remain both a sin and a crime, Panos," Amer said. He paused briefly and stared out to the sea. "Until those inside are free to return to their homes in Palestine, my work is never done. You should see their faces. They've lost dignity, pride, their identity. Thank you for your help in securing funding. Sadly, the crowding, squalor, and miserable resources have not changed since 1948."

"I will always support your efforts, Amer, you'll always be my best friend. You know that you can contact me anytime I might help more." Amer embraced Panos' shoulders.

"I'm forever grateful, friend," Amer said. "I'll miss these weekends with you, but I am proud in knowing what a wonderful father you've been to Kleïs, who loves you in return. The times you will have together should not be spent with me. You've been so generous sharing these weekends. But now, you and Ana should enjoy the time with Kleïs as a family."

Cherishing his vision of the children slapping the foamy water with the soles of their feet, Amer gazed at the sea's horizon, silently imploring Poseidon to offer safe passage for the girls. He sensed that what made them so beautiful in the moment was the unforgiving truth of their transience.

# I

CASABLANCA

MORROCO

JULY 2017

The birth of the Mediterranean Sea was abrupt and traumatic after a breach of the retaining wall holding back the Atlantic Ocean delivered an unrelenting surge into the deep valley, when Africa had rammed into Eurasia. The violent clashes of great civilizations that inherited the coastline left sibling cultures that continue their warring views of life. Here I am, too, thought Diana as she greeted her host in the port city, another heir to Mother Nature's harsh legacy of history.

She inhaled the pine and mint scent of eucalyptus stems cut from the nearby Bouskoura Forest, an olfactory dissonance from the toasted aromatics of the small coffee house just off Mohammed Zerktouni Boulevard. In a quiet corner far from the entrance door, Ali welcomed his visitor, dipping his head as a greeting. He smoothed his shirt and silently cursed a small stain on his white trousers as he motioned to a table in the corner. The two sat across from each other, and Ali signaled the waiter.

Diana, who was in her early fifties, was pleased that she arrived unnoticed in the North African city. She thanked Ali for providing a safe house for her and security from any who would be following or inquiring about her whereabouts. Ali offered her peace and good morning. This was Diana's third visit to Morocco in the last year aided by Ali.

Speaking softly in Arabic, she began by acknowledging his own pain, offering sympathy again for the inconsolable loss of his older brother. "Are you able to talk about this, Ali, or is the memory still too heavy?"

"It's even worse today, Diana, because it is still uncertain who triggered the explosion at the Internet café."

Diana closed her eyes briefly. This was a city that was at once charming, mysterious, and treacherous.

Ali nodded his thanks. "Your cause is very important, my friend."

"Inshallah," responded Diana. She looked directly into Ali's eyes. "Yes. God willing," replied Ali.

An elderly waiter quietly presented small cups of espresso, then softly retreated. Diana reviewed her efforts in hospitals in the West Bank, a coincidental encounter with a gifted colleague whom she planned to meet again soon, and the talented international team the two had assembled to execute the clandestine project. She hoped to remain in Morocco for only a few days and, with some assistance, find a flight out of the city.

"We have so much in common, you and me," Ali said. "I'm so sorry about your own loss. You must continue your sister's work, complete her task. I understand more than most what you're going through, the pain and your desire to honor her memory."

The unyielding grief in her eyes prompted Ali to change the subject. "Tell me more about your work in Palestine at the hospitals?"

"Thank you, Ali. So many deserving people with so few resources, essentially prisoners in an occupied land, and for too long needing us physicians.

"In my mind Gaza is an open-air concentration camp. In the morning I assist in the operating rooms delivering anesthesia, but in the afternoons and early evenings I do what I can in the emergency departments, clinics for women, on the overcrowded wards, developing strategies to secure medications for our people."

"And do you see your mother and father?" inquired Ali.

Pausing to take a brief sip of coffee, Diana responded, "My father lives on the wind, arriving wherever he is needed to do the work, providing funding for Palestinians. I see him on short notice only occasionally in cities along the Mediterranean. My mother is more reclusive and rarely leaves her home near Athens. I've not seen her in years. That's what the Fates have designed for me."

"And your new colleague has needed skills for your task abroad?"

"Yes, and a dedicated champion."

"I wish you well," he said, scanning the clientele to see who might be paying attention to them, then fixing his gaze back on her. "There are dark forces in this city. You would be wise to stay in hiding until you are prepared to leave. From the shadows, eyes peer into space, waiting to notice a stranger, trading money for their information, which they make available to surveillance operatives of any shade. They sell secrets in the Kasbah to the highest bidder in the market, possessing neither shame nor loyalty to any cause – only greed."

Placing his cup down, he surveyed people walking by the front door to the coffee house. "Though you slipped quietly from your home in Palestine unnoticed, there are always footprints in the sand for patient followers, eager to pursue, even after a haboob." No Saharan dust storm could erase every track.

"I suggest you remain in our beautiful city for only a few days to be sure to complete your new mission safely. I have arranged hiding, food, and secure communication needs," Ali said, pausing to offer Diana time to ask any questions.

"The screen of security will allow no light to pass, I promise you that. You are an invisible guest of our land, with a critical mission." He stared at the ceiling as though transported to another time, another place. "You cannot be too careful in our business. I've learned some bitter lessons." He gazed directly at her.

A woman in her early 30s entered the coffee shop. She surveyed the faces of the clientele now filling all but one of the tables, as if seeking a friend, then asked to be seated. She was wearing a black headscarf, dark glasses, a gray long-sleeved buttoned-up shirt, and a long black linen skirt. Nothing about her distracted the customers conversing quietly over morning coffee.

Ali recognized the regulars at the coffee shop, but this latest arrival was new to him. In response to a question from Diana about the woman, Ali noted that the dark glasses were a European designer's and that she didn't wear a wedding ring. She wore sandals with braided rope ties, most likely made in France.

The stranger placed her sunglasses on again, seeming to move her focus from one set of customers to another, before fixing on Ali and Diana, but only for a few seconds. Appearing uninterested in anyone specifically, she removed her dark glasses again to inspect the menu, then focused back to the front of the coffee shop and to the palm trees lining the street.

Diana saw that Ali was unsettled by the young woman's arrival. He suggested that Diana finish her coffee and leave with him by the back door. "Just a precaution," he said apologetically.

As Ali and his guest rose to leave, the lady with the headscarf stood up, gently pushed the chair aside and walked slowly towards them in the direction of the back door.

Ali nudged Diana into the kitchen in front of him, asking her to continue, then turned to the woman in soft pursuit and inquired in Arabic what she wanted.

She smiled and said that she thought she recognized the attractive lady with him, perhaps an old friend from school.

Ali responded politely, "Of course, please come with me, and we'll get you together."

As both passed through the moving doors to the kitchen, Ali swiftly turned to the woman, clawed her face with his strong fingers, forcing her head violently against the wall, and with confident precision, thrust a long knife into her abdomen, holding her mouth so that she could not call out. Three kitchen workers, as in a drill, left the area and entered the back of the café to sit together at a nearby table.

When she stopped resisting, Ali carried the limp body to the back door of the café. In the alley he waved for a colleague driving a taxi and then emptied the contents of the woman's pocket book onto the ground. A small handgun, a badge, and an encrypted message on her cell phone confirmed her role with Interpol. He placed the agent's body onto the back seat next to him and motioned for Diana to sit in the front passenger side, calling for the driver to depart at once.

# II

PALO ALTO

CALIFORNIA

Two fellows, one resident, one intern, and three medical students struggled to keep up with Jake Evan's pace, swiftly coursing the hallway to the Stanford University hospital's ICU.

"Good morning, Kim." He addressed the unit's head nurse. "How's my favorite patient, Karen Liu?"

"Alert and oriented. Getting her appetite back and I think stable enough to transfer to the ward. Her mother is bedside and wants to thank you for recognizing the cause of her fever and stiff neck so readily." Smiling wryly, she added, "I told her, any medical student would have recognized this as quickly!"

"Thanks, Kim. I love you too."

Cleansing his hands with alcohol foam from a dispenser in front of the room, he entered with his retinue of learners.

"Good morning, Karen. Good morning, Mrs. Liu. How are you doing?" He stood by the smiling patient.

"Much better, Dr. Evans. No headache today."

"Wonderful. You look comfortable. May I examine you briefly?"

She nodded.

Jake grasped both sides of her head gently and slowly flexed and rotated her neck. "No longer stiff, great!"

He pulled down the skin below each eye exposing the red conjunctiva of the lower lids. "No petechiae that helped me think of meningococcus," he said, referring to the ruptured tiny capillaries accompanying the infection. He proceeded to examine her mouth, listen to her lungs and heart and palpate her abdomen. Her arms and legs had no rash, and she had no neurological deficits.

Pointing to one of his fellows, Dr. Stan Ralcow, he said, "What's the plan for the patient?"

"Continue ceftriaxone for a total of seven days, monitor her for any neurological issues, treat her close contacts with two days of rifampin and arrange for follow up in your clinic one week after discharge. In the meantime we'll follow her vital signs and CBC. Her recent blood cultures are negative. We suggest quadrivalent meningococcal vaccine after convalescence."

"Excellent, Stan. Karen, do you or your mother have any questions?"

Karen shook her head. Mrs. Liu said, "We're so grateful for your help, doctor. I never thought I'd see a doctor stay with a patient all night long to be sure she did well."

"My pleasure. I will have one of my colleagues see Karen in the clinic, since I'll be taking my family on a trip to Spain. We leave in two days."

"Have a great trip, doctor. You deserve the time away," said Mrs. Liu. Jake was surprised by her hug but embraced the petite woman, his frame a good foot taller than hers. He smiled over her head at his gallery.

In the hallway, Jake peppered his team with questions to keep them alert, pointing to each in succession. "What are the four most important causes of bacterial meningitis? Which one is most serious? What is the best empirical therapy, pending culture results? How do the bacteria get to the central nervous system from the upper respiratory tract where they first attach themselves? What vaccines are currently available?"

They fired off satisfactory responses, and Jake thanked them all, shaking hands with each and fixing his eyes on theirs individually, admonishing them to keep reading and keep talking to patients.

"Now, go to the lab and examine the Gram stain of the spinal fluid and then the culture plates. You can tell me later today how you would recognize the meningococcus on each test."

They scurried away to the microbiology section of the hospital, as Jake headed to his office. Passing by the dean of the school, Lawrence Martin, Jake smiled. "Good morning, Larry."

"Hi Jake, you look especially prosperous." He pointed to his starched white shirt and absent tie.

"That bad, Larry?" Jake said with a widened smile. He had stopped wearing ties two years before to minimize bacterial transfer to patients. He wondered if the dean just now noticed.

"In all seriousness, Jake, congratulations on your invitation to be chair of medicine at the University of Chicago. I hope you turn it down but understand if you go."

"Thanks, Larry. I'm going to think about it for about two weeks before responding. I hope our family vacation in Europe will clear my head, and Deb and I can discuss this leisurely in Barcelona."

"Good luck then, Jake."

Jake continued down the hall and crossed the courtyard to his office, when he received a page to the office of the hospital's CEO, Cliff Crawford.

Ushered into the CEO's office by the assistant, Jake waved to Cliff, "Good morning, Sir."

"Hi Jake. Please have a seat. I will only hold you a few minutes but wanted to thank you personally for your epidemiological work, solving the mystery of bloodstream infections among surgical patients exposed to a new but contaminated endoscope. Great work!"

"Thanks, Cliff. Our infection-control nurses did a great job collecting the data. I just did some statistical analyses."

"Well when you get back from Spain, we'd like to have a small reception for your team to thank you."

"Very kind, Cliff. Thanks." He rose to leave and noticed a small brown area on the back of Cliff's hand. "How long you had that?"

"A few weeks, I think."

"Probably nothing, but I suggest you see Julie Masters, our dermatologist. Say I sent you. If it's anything serious, you will have gotten to it early."

"Okay. I'll call over for an appointment today, thanks."

In the faculty dining room, Jake stopped for coffee and walked to a small table to sit down for a few minutes. Placing his cup on the table, he noticed Rita DiGuissipe entering the room and walked over to give her a big hug. Jake tried not to stare into her beautiful eyes. She did have the most gorgeous eyes and smile.

"Hi Rita, what's new over in cardiology?"

"Not much. A few murmurs here and there, some congestive heart failure, unknown causes for chest pain," she answered as she reached around to grasp Jake's arm, causing him to hold her closer.

"Well, you look great, Rita." He meant it. He always noticed more than her pretty face.

"You too, my friend. Let me grab my cup and join you. I have a few minutes before I leave for the cath lab."

Her pager buzzed, she apologized for leaving right away and hugged Jake again.

Absolutely lovely, thought Jake, watching her legs move sprightly as she rushed away. The soft sway of her hips reminded Jake of Elizabeth Foster, a senior agent with the United Kingdom's security service, MI-5. He had become deeply enamored of her when they worked together two years earlier on a bioterror threat in London. Some women imprint themselves on your mind forever.

Jake decided to carry the coffee to his office and call home.

"Hi, honey. How's your day so far?"

Deborah Evans was ebullient. "Great! I had a good workout at the gym, bought some walking shoes for our trip, purchased a book on places to see in Barcelona, and sent an email to Mary Rose in England to say how much we look forward to seeing them and their children."

Jake was relieved Deb sounded upbeat. "Wonderful, Deb. This'll be a great family time together, with warm memories for the kids and us. I just want some quiet time to relax."

"I know, Jake, you've been working so hard in the past several months. When do you think you'll be home today?"

"Probably early. My patient load is light and none are critical. So I should see you by six. I have a few patients in the clinic and a few phone calls, that's all."

"Perfect. I'll stop by the wine store and pick up one of your favorite super Tuscans so that we can plan to be bored in Barcelona."

Jake laughed. "That'll be our travel slogan, *Bored in Barcelona!*"

# III

"**W**ho is my favorite poet, you ask ... well ... it's the tenth Muse." Raising her eyebrows in a "how about that" stance above tinted glasses with thin red frames, Diana lifted the edge of the crystal glass to her lips, sensing the slightly acidic texture of white wine with its faint peach intensity.

Without hesitation, Diana's new friend stared intensely into her eyes, "At the sight of you, my voice falters, my tongue breaks."

Diana was pleased to hear this iconic song of the ancient Greek poet.

It was fate, Diana thought, that had conspired to unite the couple a year earlier at their first meeting in Corsica. Diana had noticed Kleïs – her strong shoulders and striking features – before the opening ceremony. They were then seated together, along with Francisco, a compatriot who owned a small bodega in Barcelona, whom Diana knew from previous projects helping the cause. It appeared Kleïs did as well.

"Kleïs, this is Diana, an anesthesiologist who dabbles in molecular biology, when the need arises," said Francisco. "And Diana, meet Kleïs, a university professor of Greek language and a doctor of computer science and all things digital. I believe the two of you may find you have much in common."

Diana was doubtful, yet sitting next to Kleïs for the opening remarks, the conversation flowed. A bond formed quickly and resolutely as those built on a shared quest for political change sometimes do.

After the introduction each mentioned that in their childhood their fathers spoke of special friends with the same names, and they explored the pathways of their younger lives. They determined that they knew each other as children. Neither woman could recall the specific details of the time on vacation but cherished their fathers' recollections. Who could imagine, thought Diana, that a few brief encounters as youthful friends building sand castles on a beach in Mykonos would blossom decades later on another Mediterranean island. With an earlier afternoon adjournment in the meeting on day two, Diana invited Kleïs to a nearby café, said by Corsican attendees to serve good food and wine.

Their mutual interest in Homer, Plato, the naked truth of Constantine Cavafy's poems, and now the lyrical poet whose work focused on longing and love forged a union of both purpose and passion. Diana had never loved a woman this way, eager to explore both her mind and her body. The natural current of their relationship carried them in that direction. Diana yielded to its pull.

In the year since the initial meeting, they had not seen each other but often exchanged letters and less frequently emails. Diana especially cherished the tender words in the handwritten notes, sometimes accompanied by books by Greek authors and poets, and at other times by compact discs featuring folk music from Crete. On her birthday Diana opened a large box containing fragrant hyacinths "to recall Apollo's love."

Diana spent lonely evenings before sleep thinking of Kleïs, longing to touch and taste her, anticipating a next meeting in Corsica, where they promised to return. Unsure of how this distant and intense romance would evolve, Diana focused on the adventure and exploration ahead.

It was Diana who introduced the idea of conducting business together, and, over the year, in encrypted messages, they had made steady strides in the architecture of a plan that would surprise and intimidate their enemies, aided by an international team of uniquely talented operatives committed to the project. The frightening consequences of a potentially successful plot managed to fan the embers of unfulfilled sexual tension.

With Ali's recent help Diana had arrived safely in Ajaccio from Casa Blanca a few days earlier. Yesterday's anticipation had yielded to today's plan to meet for wine and unabashed exploration of feelings.

Diana studied Kleïs's vibrant blue eyes, her dark hair barely falling just over the ears, and marveled at her flawless bronze skin. A powder-blue necktie and brilliant white shirt perfectly matched a neatly pressed, pinstripe suit that encased Kleïs' body with all of her classical features. Kleïs told Diana that dressing like a man might serve them well in their mission, adding that she also felt an increased sexual excitement generated by appearing in such masculine fashion with Diana. Diana's curiosity was heightened.

The late May breeze embracing the coastal town outside of Ajaccio blushed soft and warm on the skin, brimming with promise. The raised café patio with ample space was an ideal venue for quiet conversation. Kleïs had suggested an imported bottle of Rebola from the Greek island of Kefalonia to celebrate. Noting the selection, the waiter, who spoke

French to the foreigners, offered an assortment of cheeses made of goat or sheep milk – casqio veghjo, casqio merzu, and brocciu. Diana observed the handsome man with brilliantine black hair, who appeared to curry favor with the attractive couple. He recognized their language and eagerly remarked that Corsica was colonized by the ancient Greeks before the Romans arrived. She smiled dismissively. When the waiter left, she mentioned to Kleïs that a culture of vendettas was a part of the social contract in Corsica, and killing in the name of family honor had a history dating back to the 17th century. She imagined that none of this was lost on any of the delegates.

The three-day annual meeting of freedom fighters from around the globe attracted a range of people sharing similar passion, commitment, urgency, some frustration and hope. Diana had long been committed to helping to create a changed and better world. The historical significance of a strategic meeting held annually in this town, the birthplace of Napoleon, stirred her motivation even more.

Kleïs swirled the Rebola and took a sip, her eyes heavy. They enjoyed the vintage, slowly taking it, and each other, in.

"Would you like to walk on the beach, Diana? My cottage is close by, and I have a lovely view of the sunset."

The attentive waiter picked up the wine glasses noiselessly by the circular bases. Kleïs left money on the table for the wine and service, and Diana removed her shoes, inviting the white sand to massage the soles of her bare feet and sift between her toes. Kleïs shrugged and did the same, her hand brushing Diana's in the process. Diana smiled her consent.

Nearby a few young boys, shirtless in short pants, gripped the black handles of bound string anchoring cherry red kites erratically dancing in the cloudless sky above. Avoiding the edge of the cobblestone road, Kleïs tugged gently at Diana's hand, gesturing to the kites and sea beyond. Diana held on, startled by the warmth of her friend's hand.

A few steps later she led Diana to the white cottage. Its thick wooden door and large brass key plate stood out as peculiar, a big lock on a small treasure. It charmed her. Resting on powdery white sand, the cottage, with light blue shutters framing the single ground-floor window, sat only twenty meters from the water's edge. "The wine dark sea," said Kleïs, sweeping her arm in introduction. She unlocked the door and unhitched the black metal latch.

"Welcome to my little seaside home away from home," she said, moving aside so Diana could enter first. Diana stepped onto random-width pine flooring and looked around the room. She was pleased that the area was warm and cozy, perhaps ideal for a bachelor, tidy and sufficient. A cream-colored leather couch beckoned. A television, anchored on the opposite wall, stood ready for projecting old movies. Walking behind the living room she noticed a small kitchen with a chestnut table set for two with lemon-colored place mats, the brightness of sunshine and hope.

Kleïs led Diana up the stairs to a bedroom facing the Mediterranean Sea, with a floor-to-ceiling window exposing the view. They stood facing each other, Kleïs holding Diana's hands to warm them.

"I can't believe we're finally together. Here. Your hands are still cold. Are you okay?"

"Yes. Just nervous, I think. It's one thing to connect over texts but quite another in person."

"Let's sit and talk a while," Kleïs suggested, moving to a small settee facing the view and dipping sun. "Thank you for telling me earlier about your sister, Diana. I know it's been quite difficult for you."

"Thank you, Kleïs. I've been lost without her, but having you has helped. You remind me of her in many ways."

"Because you both worked together in the quest for change? Or because of our closeness? There's so much I want to ask you, so much we haven't been able to cover in our letters and email."

Diana knew it would take some time to explain how she and Sasha combined skills to create a designer bacterium, *Staphylococcus aureus*. They added genes that coded for broad antibiotic resistance and a gene coding for a toxin causing rapid paralysis of muscles.

"I can describe it in more detail another time."

After a moment of silence, Diana explained that the plot to kill or disable friends and supporters of Israel who were attending an international medical-legal congress was uncovered by MI-5 with help from a molecular biologist from London and a talented infectious diseases epidemiologist from Stanford University. Thus, the lives of hundreds of delegates attending the meeting – who were sympathetic to Israel's causes – were spared.

"We were in disguise at the meeting, but when the plot was discovered Sasha and I were frantic to escape capture in London as agents closed in on the congress venue. Sasha was killed after the car we were driving crashed. At the hospital I managed to elude my captors, disguised as an elderly Greek nun. In Palestine I delivered my son two years ago, the child of my lover, a London surgeon."

Kleïs embraced Diana.

As to her father's involvement in targeting Israeli leaders to avenge the deaths of so many Palestinians in the Gaza war in 2014, Diana exercised caution, hesitating to expose the deeper part of her life.

Kleïs described a strong-willed father from a Basque village who had married his Greek sweetheart when both met and fell in love on the island of Crete. Moving from this cradle of civilization only in the last decade, both parents had settled in southern France, where the father had joined a separatist group with renewed interest in splitting off the Basque territory from Spain. He repeatedly mentioned his frustrations with the slow progress and continual setbacks of the organization to Kleïs, who had vowed to support the cause. Kleïs thought that it was premature to disclose all the exciting new activities currently occupying her father's collaborators and their interests.

Diana and Kleïs met initially and had registered for last year's annual meeting of *The International Days of Corte* for companionship of like-minded individuals, an interest in learning about programs successful in gaining power over established governments, and the possibility of working on an initiative likely to succeed. Many of those attending were a part of the National Liberation Front of Corsica, a violent separatist group seeking independence from France, periodically carrying out bombings and assassinations. With varied employment backgrounds, all were nevertheless militant separatists bent on rallying each other for action. That action meant that some would die in the pursuit for a better world.

This year's focus was on destroying infrastructure with unique approaches on soft targets. Diana and Kleïs were eager to see how their own ideas matched those being presented. They had concentrated on the parsimony and elegance of their asymmetric approach to terror. Each had background talents that seemed to synergize the frightful outcome they wanted.

The two talked through the setting sun until the room was dark except for a light from the street below. Finally relaxed and warm, Diana sat close to Kleïs on a blue curved couch that looked almost purple in the twilight. She bent her knees and tucked her bare feet to the side. Kleïs gently tugged Diana's ankles close by, brushing the sand away and tenderly massaging one, then the other.

Diana turned into Kleïs, resting her head on her shoulder and her arm across Kleïs' chest. She ran her fingers across her blue tie, smoothing its length a few times before loosening its knot, and unbuttoning the starched white shirt. With that enticing cue Kleïs lifted Diana to her feet and unfastened her short sleeve blouse until it hung loosely on her shoulders. She reached around Diana's waist to release her skirt, which parachuted to the floor.

With her fingers on Kleïs' back, Diana freed up the tight cotton undershirt holding her friend's taut breasts beneath. Diana ran both hands through Kleïs' coarse, violet hair. She pressed her own breasts to the breasts of this beautiful person and gasped, charged by the newness of the touch.

"I want to feel every pleasure together," Kleïs said. "Every place I visit, I want to share it with you. Have you ever been to Alexandria, Diana, the birthplace of Cavafy?" She pressed her lips onto Diana's neck and continued, "If not, we should travel there together some time. It is so romantic."

"I've never been. I did study his poetry in school near Athens. I would enjoy sharing the experience," said Diana, continuing the unscripted ceremony of complete disrobing, the street lamp's soft light shadowing curves and valleys.

Diana stood with her hands on Kleïs' hips. Kleïs' hands rested on Diana's. Diana suddenly thought of Sasha and the comfort they had given each other. The emotional closeness with Kleïs was remarkably similar. Diana's eyes welled up unexpectedly, as she recalled the loss of an all too brief life. "Everything is okay," she assured her friend, "These are tears of joy."

As though to say no words were necessary, Kleïs softy pressed her forefinger onto Diana's lips and added, "I know it was very special to be so close to your sister." She sealed the understanding with a tender kiss, pressing her closer onto the edge of the bed.

# IV

BARCELONA

THE NEXT DAY

Inside Tio Pépe's, the syncopated drumming from a sudden midday rainstorm against the tin roof was drowning out all but the loudest conversations between customers. At a small table with two chairs and a green bottle labeled *Ron* resting conspicuously near the proprietor, Eduardo perspired heavily while explaining to Ramón that he needed another two days to pay for the drugs he had acquired from Ramón's business colleague. Eduardo wiped sweat from his balding hairline onto his dirty jeans, his round face flushed with fear.

"I am just a middleman," he pleaded, "but a man of honor." He blurted out explanations: that his buyers had promised that they would pay up in a day or two, that he had trusted them completely because they had made similar purchases twice before, without incident. Eduardo's gaze darted back and forth. Ramón was used to the darting.

"You afraid to look me in the eyes? You have something against tattooed eyes?" Ramón stared into Eduardo's face with a locked gaze. He recalled his own terror when he looked into the eyes of his fellow banda, before they injected the fluid that dyed the whites of his eyes with indigo ink as initiation into the prison gang. Their reputation among prisoners for their menacing gaze was not overrated. It was during his incarceration that he became an inveterate weight lifter and martial artist.

Ramón put two shot glasses on the table, offering Eduardo a drink of rum and urging him to relax, not to worry. "What are friends for?" Ramón then took out a handkerchief, folded it in half and dabbed the damp forehead of his business companion, who raised his right hand in a gesture of thanks.

"How is your family, your wife, Maria, and your shapely daughter Nadia? Is she off to university next fall?"

Eduardo nodded, irritated by the focus of this discussion and choosing not to elaborate.

"You are a very fortunate man, Eduardo. Let's toast to your health, your comely ladies and their pleasant fortunes ahead." Both men downed the contents of the small glasses in one swallow.

Placing his empty shot glass upside down on the table, Ramón stood. He shrugged his shoulders and threw his hands up in the air, exasperated that several customers entering the newspaper and magazine store had crowded the front area, precluding a private conversation. He pointed to a back room where the two could discuss plans more discreetly to resolve the current problem.

Eduardo led the way with a sardonic smile.

Ramón followed, briefly glancing back to give a chopping hand signal to his cashier indicating that no one was to disturb him. The cashier pointed his index finger back to Ramón, acknowledging that they had an understanding.

As Ramón closed the heavy metal door to the back office and an adjacent storage area, the newly engaged lock clicked loudly. Ramón smiled, noting that the sound startled Eduardo. A small desk lamp faintly illuminated the room which had a pungent smell of turpentine hanging in the air. Ramón grasped a two-foot long piece of lead pipe that had been resting by the door frame. Without warning, he slammed the pipe against Eduardo's right knee. Eduardo began to whimper and stagger. With lightning speed Ramón smashed the outside edge of the left knee, and the obese man collapsed. With his head facing the floor, he lay still.

When Eduardo appeared to waken, Ramón picked up a thin wooden dowel and brusquely turned the man's head to the side, placing one end of the dowel into his ear canal. Raising his left hand, he hammered the dowel with the pipe, piercing the ear drum and causing Eduardo to scream savagely and collapse once more onto the floor.

After a minute, as the wounded man seemed to regain consciousness, Ramón grasped the front of Eduardo's sweatshirt and dragged him to the edge of the room, where he sat him up against the far wall, as though to comfort him. Ramón focused his purple eyes on his victim and said softly, "Amigo, you have until tomorrow morning at 9:00 to find the money. I do hope you're listening carefully. Comprendes? I am so sorry to cause you any discomfort, my friend, but you need to show more discipline in this business."

"Si. Si, Ramón," stuttered the injured man. "Lo siento." Blood trickled from his ear canal and down his jaw. He covered his face.

Ramón helped Eduardo to his feet, brushing the dust off his sweatshirt and pointing to a large eyehook in the wall by which he could pull himself all the way up. Ramón then fixed his eyes on Eduardo's and gave a soft slap to his cheek. "You are a smart man, Eduardo, and I'm sure you won't let me down again. Now do what you need to do, and then be sure to take some time with your family tonight, the lovely ladies in your life. They need you and need protection. There seems to be a lot of violence in Barcelona these days."

Eduardo hobbled out of the building ignominiously into the wet afternoon. Ramón watched Eduardo limp to his left for a few paces, pause for some time, and then retrace his steps to continue to the right. He appeared to have gathered his bearings and erratically edged up the sidewalk, where he entered a late-model black Volkswagen bug.

Just then Ramón's cell phone buzzed. He recognized Diana's cell number. The caller spoke in English, "Is Hermes free for an appointment?"

Ramón responded affirmatively, "He is on his way, expecting you. Can I take a message?"

"I have been to Corsica and now back in the White House and need some assistance. Can you provide service this afternoon"?

"For you, of course … Claro que si! Will you want help from Poseidon?"

"I prefer to have Icarus for guidance, given my special interests in a briefer travel time. Of course I'll send details by the usual way as auspicious timing arises. Muy amable, you are very kind, my friend. Grácias!"

"De nada, amiga. No problem." Ramón understood what was needed to arrange safe transportation in short order. It was only a two-hour flight.

# V

BARCELONA

TWO DAYS LATER

I n June, the Avenida Colombo in Barcelona bustled in early evening much like the Champs-Élysées in Paris, thought Jake Evans, but the street seemed to brim with more extroverts than are habitually seen in French cafés. Despite some lingering fatigue from the overnight flight, he and his family sought a comfortable outdoor venue for their first dinner in Spain. After a cab ride to the center of town, they had strolled 10 blocks from La Rambla, walking past the Barcelona Museum of Contemporary Art, the Mercat de la Boqueria, with its huge selection of mushrooms, Escribá with patisserie-stuffed windows, and La Manual Alpargatera, specializing in espadrilles. Periodically peering into a Mediterranean restaurant or two, the family was embracing all that the ancient Catalonian city had to offer.

Jake asked the family to remain briefly outside of the Carrero jewelry store. He entered hastily and quickly returned with a gold necklace for his wife, Deb, to celebrate their European trip. He had ordered a piece by her favorite designer before leaving California.

"That's beautiful, Jake! Thank you." She kissed him, spun around beaming like a child and linked her arm in his to walk down the avenue.

"Over here, honey," said Deb, excitedly pointing to an outdoor restaurant with the coral sunlight splashing over brilliant white tablecloths. Jake couldn't help but notice two women in animated discussions, each in their thirties and each with thin skirts resting at tanned mid-thigh. Deb teasingly repeated, "Over *here*, dear."

Brice and Tracy ran to lay claim to a table with the best seats for people-watching. Jake remembered the teens racing as young children, Brice always a few steps ahead of his younger sister. Both were excited that each setting had beautiful crystal for water, flutes for the bubbly Spanish cava as well as individual stemware for dinner wines, both tinto and blanco. Surely, no one would card them here in exotic Spain. Palo Alto, with all its restrictive rules excluding teenagers from public drinking, was a world away.

The friendly waiter recognized the quartet as American and used his best English to take drink orders. Jake and Deb chose Madeira, and Brice and Tracy ordered the Sangria. The waiter pointed to a large flat screen monitor where the soccer game between England and Spain was being carried live.

"Salud! y Gracias," said Brice, raising his glass to family members, proudly offering a sample of his language skills.

"Salud!" came the unison response.

Jake had arranged the holiday in part to make amends for his long absence doing epidemiological detective research. That work had kept him in London and made him miss a special anniversary. He wasn't responsible for the delay, but Deb had never erased her suspicion about his relationship with the attractive MI-5 agent he had told her about afterward. His microbiological colleague from the U.K, Chris Rose, had helped him in that investigation, and Jake had arranged for Chris and family to join in on this holiday.

Two boisterous Spaniards in their late teens passed the café, unsteady and pushing each other. Both boys appeared to be mildly intoxicated. As they wandered by Jake's table, one stopped and put his hand on Deb's neck admiring her necklace. He tried to unlock it.

Jake sprang into action and grabbed the boy's arm, twisting it until the boy fell over. The other boy ran, and Jake let the would-be thief go, not wanting to create an international incident.

"Good work, Dad," said Brice.

"Thank you for saving my beautiful necklace, Jake," said Deb. "But I'm glad he didn't have a knife or gun."

"Oh, my God, Dad. That was amazing!" said Tracy.

"Well," said Jake sheepishly, "your mom is right. I could have been hurt. It's not wise to get into a street fight, especially in a foreign country. Probably not my smartest move."

The waiter rushed out, exclaiming that he had seen the entire incident. He apologized over and over again while he took their order. A nervous pounding persisted in Jake's chest alongside relief that he didn't have to fight a drunken teen. Jake asked the waiter to bring him a scotch on ice before taking orders.

The restaurant specialized in an array of interesting and authentic Catalonian food, unfamiliar to Jake and his family. They sought advice from the young waiter. Good food and wine were important to Jake and Deb, the key to their entertaining at home and to their enjoyment on vacations. The waiter suggested beginning with sardines in escabeche, with paprika and laurel leaves. The teens chose jamon iberico for the main course, and Jake and Deb opted for tiger shrimp, gabas, with a side of chipirones or savory baby squid. All four shared the various dishes, and the waiter suggested a Muga white rioja to accompany the seafood. But when the children requested a second round, Deb gave a brief scissors motion with her hands and softly countered, "Basta, por favor, enough please." Each teen reluctantly settled for sparkling water.

As the wait staff cleared the plates from the main course, the football game was interrupted with a breaking news item. There had been an explosion at the main railroad station in Barcelona. The word *terrorista* scrolled across the bottom of the screen, and Jake anxiously asked the waiter to translate.

"Señor, it seems maybe twenty people was killed instantly and another fifty is injured. It could be accidental, but the police is worried about terrorism these days, and there is always concern for chemical or biological release."

Hearing "release," Jake paid the bill promptly, leaving a generous *propina* for the waiter, who thoughtfully arranged for a cab. Jake directed the cab driver to the hotel where he knew he could view CNN Europe on the English Channel to clarify things. The hotel was over twenty kilometers from the train station, but Jake could not free himself from a chilling sensation of dread.

In the circular hotel lobby small clusters of guests were speaking Italian, Spanish, and Arabic. All seemed obviously disturbed by the news of the explosions at the train station. Jake noticed two couples pressing iPhones tightly to their ears, apparently whispering nervously to friends and families about the explosion.

A few minutes later, in the second floor mini suite, Jake and Deb watched CNN Europe from the couch while their two teens sat on the floor, glued to the updates. CNN was now offering continual if not repetitious coverage of the bombing incident. Immediate speculation was that the Basque separatist group, *ETA*, was becoming active again. Spanish elections were looming, and a meeting of the American and British prime ministers with their counterpart from Spain and other national dignitaries was to occur in only a few days. The anti-terrorist, first-response team could identify no traces of weapons of mass destruction. The station reported that the government was almost positive that no evidence for nuclear waste products was present, and significant amounts of chemical or biological dispersal could be ruled out.

Ninety minutes later Jake received a call from Chris. "Hi, Jake, we just landed and are taxiing to our gate after circling for thirty minutes, I guess due to heavy traffic. How are you? How's the hotel?"

"Our suite is comfortable, and the view is spectacular. But listen, Chris! Just two hours ago a large explosion caused the deaths of about twenty people in the railroad station here in Barcelona. The question lingers regarding a coincidental release of a biological or chemical agent. Insist that your cab driver make a wide arch far from the train station to get to the hotel."

Chris responded soberly, "Bloody mess! Sorry. Well, thanks, Jake, we'll be sure to emphasize avoiding the train station. Let's meet as soon as we check in."

Ten minutes later the phone in the room rang, and a man asked to speak to "Dr. Jake Evans, a medical doctor from Stanford University."

"I am Dr. Evans." The line went dead. Jake shrugged his shoulders and slowly hung up the receiver. The front desk knew his name and had his address in Palo Alto, but he hadn't remembered telling anyone he was an M.D. Or that he worked at Stanford. Perhaps he had mentioned it to the inquisitive porter.

Sixty minutes afterwards, Chris, Mary and their two teenage daughters, Chloe and Jane, arrived. The children cloistered themselves in one side of the suite while the adults caught up and began to address the recent bombing. Still feeling a bit unsettled, Jake briefly mentioned the caller who had hung up as soon as he responded.

Mary tried to be reassuring. "ETA usually has specific targets; they hit once, and it's over. They've never been involved in weapons of mass destruction," she said.

"What exactly is ETA? What do they want?" asked Deb.

"From everything I've read, Deb, they are a militant wing of the Basque people, who basically want independence from Spain." Chris went on to describe ETA as the oldest terrorist group in Europe and still active after fifty years, but thought to be considerably weaker than they were twenty years before. Not long ago, they made a public statement that they would halt violence. At least that was what the media in the U.K. reported. They have a different culture and language from the Spanish, even different from the Catalonians living here in Barcelona. The Catalonians argue for independence also, but they are not terrorists."

"This should blow over quickly except for the victims and their poor families," he reassured Deb.

The television news was interrupted with an announcement that among the dead were two American and three British staff members of their respective embassies. Speculation expanded on a possible motive and whether this was a random event by a disgruntled citizen or a targeted act of foreign terrorism. Although most of the focus was on ETA, there were other considerations and references to the mass killing of children in Norway in 2011 and the U.S. in 2012, as well as to various terrorist incidents involving Al Qaeda and ISIS. There were also brief references to terror incidents in France in 2016. The TV reporter noted that approximately twenty people from the rail station incident required hospitalization without physical injury, the psychological effects of terror already palpable.

The phone rang again. As Jake picked up the receiver, a man with a Spanish accent spoke in clipped English, "All Americans should leave Spain at once."

# VI

A t the Barcelona General Hospital situated close to the international airport, Dr. Jose Morales was in charge of the city's leading trauma emergency room. With black ruffled hair and a thick beard, he moved confidently through the hallways where an urgent triage system had been set up. He inquired about every patient, the type of injury and their general status. In a turbulent sea of pale-blue operating room scrubs, physicians and nurses responded as though commanded by a seasoned officer in a well-rehearsed scenario. Morales knew the command and control medical role well and listened attentively, one case at a time.

"Twenty-two-year-old woman with shrapnel involving most of the left calf, blood vessels lost to major destruction, preparing for transfer to OR 5. Likely AKA." So young for an above the knee amputation, he thought.

"Twenty-nine-year-old man with an open abdominal wound and intra-abdominal hemorrhage. Ruptured spleen. Currently stabilizing with IV fluids, blood and antibiotics. Will move to OR 9 as soon as the blood pressure is up."

"Fourteen-year-old boy. No direct injury, but blood sugar high at 515 milligrams per deciliter and in diabetic ketoacidosis. Somewhat dehydrated. He'll be all right with some saline and insulin. Says he hasn't had this problem for over five years."

"Seventy-year-old man with cardiomyopathy found down at the station. No obvious direct injury, although he has some chest pain. Chest film ordered. Main problem is a refractory tachycardia with erratic heartbeat at 120 – 175 beats per minute. Cardiac enzymes pending. No evidence of an MI on EKG. Working on stabilizing this rhythm and interrogating his pacemaker." Good news, thought Morales, no true heart attack from coronary artery occlusion.

"Nine-month-old baby with head abrasions. Awaiting head CT imaging, but he is stable. The mother is fine. Should be able to discharge soon." There but for the grace of God, thought Morales.

"Forty-one-year-old woman, essentially DOA. We tried CPR and intubation to no avail. There was no electrical heart activity. Very sad. We've just called off the code, and we'll talk to the family."

"Another diabetic out of control, and two other cardiac patients – none with traumatic injuries. We've called in Psychiatry to help us."

One by one, Morales went to each victim's bedside and received the updates, observing every patient directly, offering clinical suggestions to the younger physicians who were often expressing uncertainty, reassuring family members of patients likely to do well, assiduously avoiding clichés when the outcomes looked serious, making sure that no patient was left unattended, and assisting victims of multiple injuries. Thirty-two had been referred to his ER alone, with others dispersed to various nearby hospitals.

Morales kept notes on all the train station victims, knowing that his administrator and the press would want details. How many in all, how many died, details about the injuries, the ages of the patients, how many needed surgery. This was not the first time Morales had responded to a medical crisis, but this was the biggest.

His first disaster had occurred during medical school, a bus crash full of tourists careening off the road down a thirty-foot rocky ravine. Ten of the victims came to his university's emergency room within twenty-five minutes, moaning in pain from multiple fractures, internal injuries, and the disorientation that accompanies unexpected random tragedies. Morales was assigned to start IV fluids while his role model, Professor Carlos Cabazudo, quickly triaged the victims to immediate surgery or resuscitation. After efficient questioning and examination, he administered narcotics for pain, requested blood for measurement of hemoglobin levels and electrolytes, and systematically rounded on all victims until they had stable vital signs, went to the OR, or were admitted to the floor. That night José Morales decided that the ED was his calling, his career choice, his medical home.

In recent training updates on response to terror, instructors emphasized that Emergency Department security was valuable for everyone – the first responders, injured patients, the families and friends. It was important to take follow-up threats out of the equation. He called for a major increase in security to be stationed not only at the ED entrance but also within the rooms and now in the over-crowded hallways of the Emergency Department.

Nurses and physicians clustered in chairs in the circular space at the center of the ED, their gaze intermittently focused on computer screens, which listed the names and bed assignments or hallway locations of each patient, their age and chief complaints. In the periphery were nineteen examination rooms. When the demand exceeded nineteen, the hallways between the central space and exam rooms overflowed with more stable patients on gurneys being attended to by nursing staff.

The ED was noisy with physicians' orders, the cacophony of nurses communicating with frightened patients and their demanding relatives, the sirens of incoming ambulances and police personnel barking orders, insisting that only one family member accompany each victim in the ED area. The high-pitched beeping from cardiac monitors, harsh blowing of respirators, and constant cell phone pings added to the chaos. Outside the ED the large waiting room had been transformed into a primary triage area, with one nurse and one physician taking brief histories and vital signs, quickly assessing the physical damage. Grief counselors had begun to assemble to help family members of injured and dying patients and those in need of stress reduction.

Morales glanced at his notes to update the injury statistics: a total of thirty-six patients, eight deaths, seven still in the operating room, two still in the hallways, and all nineteen rooms occupied. Five of the thirty-six had minimal or no physical injury but had underlying heart issues that stress seemed to exacerbate; two diabetics had blood sugar levels out of control unrelated to injury. Perhaps they had forgotten to take their insulin after the explosion.

Of the eight people who had died, two were children ages four and nine, three were adults between ages sixteen and thirty, and one each in their forties and sixties. Two of the survivors would likely have AKAs from severe lower leg injuries, and four would likely be discharged later that night.

Morales would make it an all-nighter, probably sleeping at the hospital for a few hours in the morning before making a decision to go home or continue to stay in the ED if needed. His next responsibilities were to update his administrator, represent the hospital to news media at midnight as requested, and call his wife, Queta, to see how his two teenage daughters were doing. He would ask her to give them an extra hug for him tonight, incidents like this reminding him how quickly events can hijack well-being, how suddenly fragile a robust life could become. Professor Cabazudo used to quote from his own role model from the U.S., Professor Frank Abboud, "Health is the crown on the head of the well, visible only to the sick." How fortunate he was, he thought, to have learned key lessons from a wise mentor, to be in a field where wisdom is passed from one generation of physicians to the next.

First he would update the administrator. Morales found speaking with Señor Lope Padilla, the hospital's administrator for the last decade, difficult. The word on the street was that Padilla envied those with a medical degree and sought physicians' approval, yet in his insecurity around doctors, he was often a bully. Much of his phrasing had the lexicon of military commanders, giving the staff an impression that Padilla was a wannabe general as well.

In every crisis at the hospital Padilla would set up a command and control room on the administrative wing of the top floor, insist on hourly updates, and sign all the broadcast email alerts to the entire staff. The emails never mentioned the names of the physicians or nurses actually doing the work. Instead he would state that "my doctors and my nurses are following hospital protocol and continually updating me here in my command room."

Padilla sat behind a massive oak desk with no nearby chairs, wearing a dark brown suit, white shirt, and designer Italian tie, forcing all visitors to stand in front while he interrogated them for new information or to sit in on one of several diminutive chairs along the wall.

Morales chose to stand in front of the desk, towering over the shorter administrator.

"I want to congratulate you, Morales, for overseeing the top-rated trauma center in Barcelona. But make sure the current experience keeps us in the number one spot. I don't want to be outflanked by lesser adversaries, not in the line of fire. Understand?"

Morales nodded. The interview went better than expected, perhaps because of his imposing physical presence, the late hour, or a combination of both. Padilla had limited stamina, it was rumored, requiring at least eight hours of sleep each night.

Now to call home to a loving voice with unconditional support, then to repeat his review of patients in the ED, make sure Psychiatry was on board, and update the statistics.

It was disturbing to see the large number of patients and the psychological trauma suffered by several, including children and young adult victims of senseless terror. Morales hoped that this was the end, that no more terror would follow. But ineffable doubts haunted his mind, preventing peaceful respite.

# VII

Wheeling a wobbly bronze luggage cart into the room, a muscular hotel security man apologetically moved Chris and his family to a mini suite on the same floor as their American friends, saying that he was sorry it had taken so long to get the luggage. He also regretted any anxiety that the recent explosion caused the visitors. No one had an easy explanation for the blast, and assurances were offered that hotel security was already heightened as a result. The man told Chris that terror incidents brought out prejudices, and that was likely why the strange call was made to Jake. He had seen it before. Special attention would be given to foreigners. "In all likelihood, ETA is making a political statement," he said calmly.

At 3:00 a.m. the phone rang, and a man with a Spanish accent asked the question, "Are you Professor Christopher Rose of London?"

Jarred awake, Chris responded irritably, "Indeed I am, and who are you, to be calling at this hour?" The caller hung up.

Mary was able to fall back to sleep quickly, but Chris remained awake, staring at the ceiling, unnerved. He remembered that Jake, too, had a caller and that the caller had hung up. And then there was the more threatening call for all Americans to leave Spain. Surely the explosion didn't target Americans or Brits. ETA focused on Spanish authority. Were the phone calls some anti-Western pranks? A real threat? And why address us with our professional titles? Why not just our last names? Maybe some calls were from the front desk, checking to see if we were settled. Eventually yielding to fatigue, Chris closed his eyes and concluded that the following day nothing would disturb a day at the beach.

Both families met for breakfast on the ground floor of the hotel. Near the entrance to the dining area, the gurgling sound of a small fountain and the sweet fragrance of fresh-cut flowers greeted the early risers. Inside, a pleasing array of various fruit juices – orange, pineapple, papaya, guava and grapefruit – lined a serving table. The aroma of dark roasted coffee filled the room, and the table offered an assortment of sliced meats, cheeses and frittatas.

The four children found a table for themselves in the far corner of the breakfast area, beyond the listening range of their parents.

At the parents' table, Chris mentioned that the early morning news had confirmed that no weapons of mass destruction were implicated in the explosion. Although ETA was assumed to have carried out the attack, so far no one claimed responsibility. A confident hospital spokesman, a seasoned emergency room physician, gave summary statistics on all victims received at six area hospitals. Chris thought it was likely that the threats from last night's explosion were over.

Seeking to change the focus, Chris announced that he had already hired a van to drive everyone to the beach recommended by the hotel concierge. The vehicle with a full tank of petrol was parked just outside. Maps would be provided with clear directions highlighted in yellow.

Concerns about explosions and terror would be abandoned at the hotel, he emphasized; he suggested everyone avoid discussing the unnerving phone calls in front of the children.

Twenty minutes later, Chris was driving the van, heading north to the Nova Icaria beach with Jake in the front passenger side, their wives in the second row of seats with Brice, and the three girls in the back. Not a cloud could be seen in the cerulean sky. The air was pristine with a morning temperature of 75º F. Chris drove by a steep twenty-foot ravine on the passenger side of the road. "I wouldn't want to do this road in the dark," he said, gripping the wheel more tightly with both hands.

The driver of a green four-door Volvo sedan traveling behind began honking his horn. Chris waved him on. The man obliged, came alongside and seemed to growl in their direction. Chris instantly slowed down, wary of the narrow road and not wanting to make a mistake.

Seeing the single-lane highway ahead and hoping to avoid another mile of treacherous road, Chris made an abrupt left turn onto a two-lane highway, swiftly accelerating in the new direction. He examined the map a few minutes later to find an alternate route to the beach.

When they finally arrived at their destination, everyone spilled out of the van, eager for their day at the shore. From the parking lot, Chris could see the golden sand of the vast playa disappear into the mysterious, calm sea. The hotel had reserved two large green-and-white striped cabanas for changing clothes and had arranged a picnic with jamón Serrano, prepared goat cheeses, olives, whole-grain loaves of freshly baked bread, grapes, apples, peaches, and bars of dark chocolate, which the group devoured under cover of dark blue umbrellas just a few meters from the softly rolling surf.

Soon after lunch the four children joined local teenagers in beach volleyball. It appeared the Spanish boys had two goals in mind: to impress the three attractive, English-speaking girls, all of whom wore bikinis, and to outplay the only English-speaking boy. Brice's command of Spanish, his stature at six feet, and a few high net spikes, however, won them over, and within fifteen minutes unrestrained laughter erupted after each point.

———————

Deb and Mary strode down the beach to catch up on each other's lives, to reminisce about their long friendship, beginning over a decade earlier during Jake's sabbatical at the London School of Hygiene and Tropical Medicine, and to express some concerns about the bombing incident. They had exchanged emails monthly for the past 12 years and called each other every few months, sharing feelings about their families, children, their hopes and dreams.

"I hope you're not worried about the bombing incident, Deb."

"I am a little, Mary. It sometimes seems that the world is spinning out of control with terrorists emerging on all continents. We've been mostly lucky in the States since 9/11, but Americans who travel abroad feel that they have a bull's eye on the back of their shirts."

"Completely understandable. Hopefully with every passing day of the holiday, you'll be continually assured of your safety."

Both ladies were attractive in their bikinis, fit women in their mid-40s, and comfortable in each other's company. Two Spanish men in their early 50s walking in the opposite direction paused to watch the foreign women pass. "Muy hermosas," uttered one as the other gave a shake of his wrist. Mary recognized it as a sign of high approval. Both women broke out laughing.

Mary said, "Does all this bombing make you think about that anti-terrorist agent in London?" Deb had told her about Jake's possible affair with the beautiful MI-5 woman when she was engaged in foiling a plot to unleash dreaded bacteria at a medical convention.

"Maybe. I'm still jealous of that bitch. Jake cheated on me with an Italian microbiologist during his earlier sabbatical in London. I've never completely trusted him since, when he travels alone. He looks at every woman and especially the young, taut ones."

"I'd probably feel the same way in your shoes, maybe even unforgiving," said Mary. "But the truth is, it was a one night stand during the sabbatical – too much wine and not a sustained affair. That was over a decade ago. And it's hard to stop a man from looking!"

"True, but I'm still not sure he didn't have a fling with the British agent more recently, when he was last in London. He seemed convincing when he denied it. But I still considered leaving him."

"He probably didn't play with the natives that time, Deb."

Mary deeply respected Deb. She knew that before meeting Jake, Deb had called off an engagement to another man two days before the wedding when her fiancé confessed to an affair. Deb was a woman of substance.

In response to a question about her job, Deb described her career as a surgical nurse, then head nurse on a surgery ward, and in the last two years a supervisor of surgical services. "The better you get, Mary, the more you get promoted away from those activities that drove you to the profession in the first place. But the flexible hours and the pay are good. I meet the children after school. Plus, I don't have to answer to jerks who seem to rise quickly in nursing administration."

"I'm sure you're still making a difference, even if it's at a higher level," said Mary. "I'm glad your flexible hours give you time with Jake and the kids. How good for your family."

"Yes, and both children are doing well in school. Brice wants nothing to do with medicine and says he wants to go to college in the East, perhaps to study political science. Tracy doesn't seem very ambitious, but at least her grades are okay. Now bring me up to speed on you and your family."

Mary reviewed her teaching activities at the local school where she had been appointed director of the arts program. She had designed separate programs in watercolor, acrylic, and oil painting. "The girls are fine, both doing well in school and seem interested in politics for some reason. As for me, I don't have much time. I've been close to burning out and decided to train for a half marathon this year, just for me!"

"I know what you mean! I joined a book club in Palo Alto just to get out of the house for dinner and fun once a month!"

Both friends laughed out loud.

"Does Jake still like his job?"

"He loves it, and he's done well. He recently traced an outbreak of antibiotic-resistant bacteria to contaminated endoscopes. He's good and also a caring clinician. When a Stanford undergrad developed bacterial meningitis, he practically lived in the ICU for 48 hours until she turned the corner.

"How about Chris?"

"He's happy in his job, too," said Mary. "His world of microbiology is changing, more automated in the lab, and he spends a third of his time worrying about data breaches. He oversees IT security for all laboratories at Oxford. I told him he's gone from bugs to bytes."

As the women turned to retrace their steps to the cabanas, their husbands walked together away from the beach. Jake's 220-pound, athletic build with slight paunch stood in stark contrast to his friend's thin frame of 160 pounds. But the energy always seemed focused on Chris, who continually gesticulated wildly with his hands and arms.

"Now there go two great specimens of manhood," said Mary.

"It could be a lot worse," noted Deb, "they might have found two local hussies to walk arm in arm with on the beach."

"You're right, Deb. It looks as though they'll settle for a night in foreign beds with reliable women they've known for over 20 years."

# VIII

## LONDON

In a London medical clinic, the cautious professor of neurology, Nigel Harrington, had invited the patient and his wife to his windowless office lined with dark mahogany bookcases whose heavy shelves bowed from the sustained weight of obese textbooks. In a properly starched white coat, white shirt, and blue and gray striped tie, the professor was explaining the natural history of Huntington's chorea to the couple in their forties.

Periodically brushing his hand through his curly gray hair, the professor said: "Elizabeth, we have no cure for your husband's illness, and, from here on, he'll be confined to a wheelchair because of the loss of motor function in both legs. But he should not withdraw from society, his work or avocations or in fact any travel you may consider. Nevertheless, his thinking may continue to deteriorate."

He paused briefly to allow a response, taking in a deep breath while straightening his back.

Trying to focus on good news, the doctor gestured to Ian Foster's large chest and well-defined arms, and he urged his patient to continue weight training to maintain his strong deltoids, biceps and triceps. "Upper body strength will serve you well."

He listened as the patient processed all the information without any visible expression of emotion. Viewing his body language and facial expressions, Harrington was sure that his patient was devastated that his legal career was racing to a premature finish at age forty-five, the result of a genetically inherited degenerative disorder that would eventually defeat both mind and body. In general, his thinking was intact, but occasionally he experienced brief interruptions of neural transmissions and would suddenly be at a loss for words; at other times he became disoriented to place and time, wondering where he was and what part of the day he was experiencing.

Harrington asked the barrister to cite an example, and the patient recalled an incident at his sons' school where he was asked to deliver a brief talk on the life of a modern barrister. The proud boys had each taken turns for a few minutes to introduce their father, a nationally prominent legal expert on state terror.

The twenty-minute presentation was flawless, but in the question-and-answer period, when asked about the implication for Al Qaeda of the assassination of Osama Bin Laden, he froze briefly, blanking on the meaning of both Al Qaeda and Bin Laden. He panicked, yet somehow knew that he was having a brief period of amnesia. He had trained himself to respond by gazing upwards as though in deep thought.

Suddenly, to the relief of his sons, his mind revived. "The spine of Al Qaeda is broken, and healing will be slow. Nevertheless, it is premature to declare the death of the organization, and to be sure, terror in one form or another will persist. As you know even more violent groups have split off from Al Qaeda, like ISIS, and they create new havoc. As an aside, it is important for you young people to know that most terrorists are home grown. Only a minority are foreigners."

Now, as his physician said he was sorry to convey the bad news, Foster merely shrugged his broad shoulders, pressed his lips tightly together and rotated his wheelchair towards the door to leave. He then swung back one hundred eighty degrees to face his clinician.

"Doctor, I know you've done your best and that medicine, an imperfect science, sometimes comes up short. Don't give up on me; don't abandon me at any time. But also don't unnecessarily prolong a life with expensive but useless technology when that dark night arrives in earnest. I don't see myself in critical care surrounded by sisters managing tubes in every orifice for weeks on end. Are we clear?"

Professor Harrington merely nodded with respect. He had heard similar requests from many of his patients. In his 30 years of neurology he had learned to respect the autonomy of patients.

Ian Foster's wife had planned to take the entire day off from her duties at MI-5, and she and Ian chose a small restaurant at Covent Garden to have lunch. Their monthly tradition was to reserve a table for two by a window and order a salad Nicoise. Since his diagnosis, he avoided all alcohol but always invited Elizabeth to have a glass of wine. Whenever they dined together, however, she chose hot tea with lemon and sugar. They discussed his prognosis, his career plans, their mutual goals of spending more time together and as much time as possible with their two children. They always began these conversations with a bright note: both boys had been evaluated and neither had the gene that coded for Huntington's.

He picked up Elizabeth's left hand, held her fingers, gently kissing the palm of her hand, tasting the metal of her wedding ring. He recalled a warm summer evening in Regent's Park when he proposed to her. They had met only three months before when he initiated a series of evening seminars on legal aspects of terrorism to young recruits at MI-5. Previously he hadn't given marriage much thought, but this intelligent, attractive, and quick-witted woman captured his mind and his heart. She was, in a word, magical. And because he had no ten- minute interval during the day when he could not think of her, he initially thought it was an unhealthy obsession, perhaps requiring a visit to a psychiatrist. But he argued his own case to himself: this was true love, a lasting love and no brief fantasy. He needed to tell this amazing woman what she meant to him.

Ian continually envisioned her smile, her laughter, her arm around his when they walked together, his complete comfort when they talked over dinner. In response to the proposal they talked for four hours over late-evening wine. She unabashedly confided her own admiration and deep affection for him openly, without any pretensions. She had no reservations and told him so. They discussed careers, family, the desire for children, favorite books and movies, art and music, and sex. Ian suggested a holiday to know each other further.

Subsequently, on a rainy weekend in a small hotel in the southern coastal town of Brighton, they made love for the first time after an early dinner and bottle of Claret. They talked into the late night about their families, their personal aspirations, and their complete happiness together.

When they were not in bed together or sharing meals at restaurants, they went for long walks on the beach in both sunshine and rain. Periodically Elizabeth would skip ahead of him, turn her head and challenge Ian to a race. With her athletic skills she usually won, giggling at the defined crossing line and ready to embrace him, throwing her long legs around his waist, her taut arms wrapping his muscular neck.

He loved this magical woman with her flowing chestnut hair and curious smile, and he needed to spend the rest of his life with her.

Elizabeth brought him back to current events. "If nothing urgent comes my way soon, we should consider expanding our planned summer holiday in Italy," she suggested. "Until then, if I am on any assignment briefly outside of London, I want you to join me. You heard the professor's encouraging statements about travel. Please say you'll do so. We'll at least see each other every day at some time. You always remain a valid sounding board in my world of intrigue."

Ian Foster had mixed feelings about his wife's suggestion. He saw both the benefits and the drawbacks. He was plaintiff and defendant on this issue, and he wanted only a rational judgment. Of course, he wanted to spend as much time as possible with his wife, but Elizabeth had to be sure to maintain her career, since his future was uncertain, and the boys needed her as parent and financial supporter. Being able to focus on the issues at hand was paramount. When Elizabeth was on assignment, he didn't want to slow her down, risk her life, or in any way jeopardize the task at hand. On balance, however, he thought he was disciplined enough to keep out of her professional path, if she accepted a very brief foreign assignment. And Harrington had given him permission if not encouragement to travel.

"Surely I'll accompany you, Elizabeth, should we face that exciting possibility. I love you."

# IX

## BARCELONA

Jake spotted a bar down the beach and concluded that a mid-day beer and discussion of events were warranted. He and Chris found two high stools at the bar.

"We probably have a couple of hours before Deb and Mary even notice we're gone. They're probably still walking," said Jake, checking out the beer options. He ordered for both of them, "Two local drafts. That okay with you?"

"Sure, man. Thanks," said Chris.

"So, I got news about the international prize at Stanford ..."

"And ..."

"Yeah, well, it didn't go my way. My project was good, *Antibiotic Resistant Superbugs in the Hospital*. But my angry reaction to challenges from the audience at the International Congress was undisciplined and over-sensitive," Jake said. "It was good fodder for the press and unfortunately made the pages of the *New York* and *L.A. Times*, widely quoted by reporters in Palo Alto. I was the butt of humor and sarcasm for a while, and no doubt after many months of the awards committee reviews this influenced the judges. That was a low point in my career, Chris. It cost me a funded chair at Harvard. There is some recent good news. I was asked to be the chair of medicine at the University of Chicago. Still thinking about it."

Chris reminded Jake that during his visit to London two years earlier, he had been jet-lagged, sleep-deprived, and in the throes of investigating a bioterror incident. "You shouldn't beat yourself up about this, Jake, an unfortunate dicey set of circumstances. You and I have discussed this before in light of your unfounded fear of failure, if I may boldly remind you. Good luck with your new decision."

"Thanks, Chris. You're a good friend for saying that. But I can't shake the feeling of self-inflicted wounds," said Jake.

Chris updated Jake on his career. "Microbiology is so high-tech today, that only older microbiologists could identify an organism on agar. It's all chemistry and analytics. So I have become an IT microbiologist.

"I remember prof Goodner holding up a petri plate close to his nose declaring that its grape-like smell indicates pseudomonas." Chris shook his head. "No more. I've had to become a computer programmer and guide." Looking around, he added, "But that's not nearly as interesting as this crowd." They both scanned the colorful array of patrons.

*El Sed* seemed to be a social magnet for the people of the small town as well as tourists. It rested under an expansive canopy of white canvas. Men, women, couples in resort wear, business attire, bathing suits, or jeans and t-shirts shared the space on stools around the bar and at the twenty or so small tables. To Jake, it appeared that most people nearby were speaking Spanish or Catalan.

Both men ordered a second pale ale. The bartender told them it was brewed only a few kilometers away. They continued to talk about academic politics and the increasing pressure to generate funds in the wake of the global recession. Both agreed that they still had the most interesting jobs on earth.

Jake paid the bill in euros, stepped to his right and did a double take. A smiling waitress with a flowing brown ponytail, a narrow waist, and prominent breasts had removed the caps of two bottles of beer – one at a time with her teeth – for two flirtatious young men at the bar. Having first placed each bottle in front of her admiring customers, she proceeded to show her unique prowess, placing the cap aside one of her back molars, clenching down to stabilize the bottle, then lifting up quickly to release the cap from the neck of the bottle. She then licked the inside of each cap, placed her tongue back into her mouth, and loudly told the two men that the beer was "excellente." Quickly pivoting away from her approving clients, she swung her hips with an exaggerated flourish and caught Jake's admiring look. She winked at him and flung her hair over her shoulder. Jake was mesmerized.

"Check her out, Chris. She has special talents."

"I admire your taste in young ladies, Jake, but your appetite may be out of place here."

"So true, my wise friend, but no harm in scanning the menu."

On the far side of the bar the object of Jake's reverie presented a check to an attractive couple at a small table. Something about the woman seemed familiar, but he wasn't sure what it was. Jake refocused his attention to the attractive hips of the young waitress, but then again to the table she had just left. Jake's heart skipped a beat. For a moment he didn't take a breath. Then he nervously asked, "Chris, look at the two people at the fifth table down. Do you see a familiar face?"

Chris squinted behind his dark glasses and nodded. "Bloody Hell. Diana Kontos. How is that possible?" Jake was transported back to an anxious time two years earlier in London.

His brain was spinning. An international bioterrorist unleashing a bioengineered *Staph aureus* that was seconds from sickening and killing hundreds of Israeli supporters at a medical meeting in London. Is she really here?

He raced through his memory. It all began with an outbreak in London of staph infections post-operatively among patients at low risk for such surgical site infections. When he compared patients infected versus non-infected controls, the exposure to a single anesthesiologist, Diana Kontos, stood out, and law enforcement authorities seized on the information.

Yet she managed to escape into thin air two years ago. Did she resurface? Why? Had he made a mistake bringing his family?

The couple at the table with their eyes fixed on each other seemed engaged in a serious discussion. At each table setting there was a glass of sparkling water beside a small cup for espresso. The couple appeared to be Spanish, Jake thought. Each was wearing a tan baseball cap and dark glasses. The man had a slightly prominent nose and was perhaps forty-five years old with a slight build, black hair with a violet hue falling over his ears, and a face that might be considered pretty, more so than handsome. The woman, who also appeared to be in her forties, had swept-back brown hair and an inviting smile. She had a prominent dimple on her right cheek just like Diana and was a few inches shorter than her companion. They both were unaware of others around them, with a mutual serenity that gave them an appearance more like lovers than business colleagues. Pushing the cups and saucers slightly away from themselves, they seemed to be near the end of their conversation. They rose from their chairs, kissed each other's cheeks tenderly, and walked hand in hand towards the roadside away from the sea.

Jake's mind searched the hard-drive files of his experience in London. An anesthesiologist with skill in molecular biology teamed up with her twin sister, a toxicologist, to create a life-threatening chimaera – a strain of *Staphylococcus aureus* that had gene coding for tissue invasiveness, for broad antibiotic resistance, and for paralysis: a gene from the organism causing botulism was spliced into the genetics of the staph bacteria, and the victims would not be able to move a muscle, not even breathe.

But how could that person who had created a bioengineered weapon of mass terror be the same one on the beach apparently enjoying a quiet afternoon?

As the couple left the premises, Jake caught Chris's eye and raced to the table where the couple had been sitting. In his rush, Jake bumped into a waiter who was bussing a table nearby, apologized briefly, made a 360-degree turn, then went around the table to continue his pursuit. Short of breath when he arrived at the table, he grasped the white cloth serviette the woman had been using. He wrapped the glass Diana, or the woman he believed to be Diana, had held, and carried the bundle down by his side as he made his way to the edge of the bar.

"I saw them leave in a recent model tan Porsche. I couldn't see the license plate," said Chris. A waiter followed the two to the door and yelled for them to return the glass and linen. Chris ran back, begged forgiveness and gave the young man ten euros.

"If the fingerprints confirm that Diana Kontos is in Spain, MI-5 ought to know," said Jake. "I may very likely be overreacting, but that woman certainly looked like her."

Whether or not she could have anything to do with the bombing was unclear to Jake. It was difficult to accept the idea that the bioterrorist who had escaped London would be in Spain only meters away from the two physicians. It didn't make sense. Nothing was clear; but if it was Diana, she was a wanted criminal. Jake couldn't ignore the possibility of her involvement in the explosion at the train station.

"We need to call Elizabeth," said Jake, referring to the MI-5 agent who had led the forensics team tracking down Diana Kontos, her late sister, Sasha, and their conspirator, Ata Atuk. "I have her number."

Jake hadn't mentioned to Chris that he and Elizabeth had maintained an e-mail friendship over the last two years. Jake had written Elizabeth that he missed her, and she had told him the same. He picked up the phone.

"Agent Foster, here. How may I help you?"

"Elizabeth, Jake Evans. I'm with Chris Rose and our families on a holiday. But there is something more important to discuss."

"Oh, Jake, you've missed me!"

"Yes, of course. But I have to tell you something very curious."

"Curious? You want me to meet you," Elizabeth teased. "Are you in Europe?"

"Yes, but seriously, Elizabeth. Chris and I are with our families vacationing at a beach near Barcelona, and we think we saw Diana Kontos!" He paused to be sure Elizabeth heard the name. "We're not sure, but a woman we saw looked just like her. She was with a man, perhaps a local Spaniard, and they left the beach area together in a tan Porsche convertible."

With new composure, Elizabeth responded. "Jake, I haven't thought about her for several months after one of our informers confirmed her presence in Palestine. Are you sure that you've not being a little nervous, back here in Europe? I did hear of the explosion at the Barcelona train station. Is it possible that the events there are stressing you?"

"Chris and I are not a hundred percent sure. However, I've taken a glass that the woman touched. I've wrapped it in a cloth to preserve any prints and can send it expressly to you for analysis. If the prints don't match, you don't need to be involved, and we won't need you here."

The call ended with an agreement that Jake should send the glass.

"I asked about a post office and learned of one that is ten kilometers farther east down the main road," offered Chris.

"Let's take care of it now," answered Jake. He raced the rental van to the post office, secured an appropriate shipping box, surrounded the glass in bubble wrap and sent it to Elizabeth in London at MI-5. They opted to pay an enormous surcharge for a twenty-four-hour delivery.

Jake and Chris finally returned to the beach late in the afternoon six hours after they had left. Mary and Deb had made drinks and wanted to hear about their day. With the children playing in the surf, unaware of their parents' new concerns, Jake and Chris told of the bar, of seeing Diana and the shipment.

"I called Elizabeth," said Jake, noticing Deb's body language stiffen at the mention of the name. "She said Diana Kontos is most likely in Palestine but to send the glass anyway."

"I don't like the sound of this, Jake. Maybe we should get to London sooner than planned."

"Deb, they probably had too many beers, and this is all a case of unreliable witnesses. We should settle down. Let's take another beach walk tomorrow. With margaritas!" Mary's smile signaled bright optimism.

Looking at the children joyously speaking Spanish and English while leaping up between the waves, Chris suggested that they wait another 48 hours by which time the prints on the glass could surely be confirmed or not. In all probability it was likely an episode of mistaken identity.

# X

In central Barcelona, police headquarters' counter-terrorist commander, Javier Gonzalez, listened to local law enforcement officers recap the bombing at the train station. "This could be ETA, but not everything adds up," said Captain Toni Palacios, pacing the small conference room. He stood still and instead fidgeted with one of his cuff links, rubbing the silver to a high sheen.

Lost in thought, he ran through his mental index of ETA facts, recalling data from his days at the University of Madrid when he studied the group as part of his criminal psychology courses. It was Europe's longest-standing terrorist group, born around 1959 out of desperation and frustration during Franco's ruthless reign. Bilbao's university students in north central Spain were angered by the dictator's furious oppression, especially against the Basque culture. Franco focused his terror on this proud people who traced their heritage to ancient Rome. Palacios estimated that close to 1,000 deaths could be attributed to the ETA. Nearly 800 ETA members packed Spanish prisons.

"A bomb in a train station is a somewhat typical ETA activity," he said even though he wasn't completely convinced. "But it is true that ISIS or Al Qaeda likes to hit two or three times in succession as in 9/11 or the attacks in Brussels. I'm just not sure yet."

Standing by the room's expansive window, looking down on the city, Javier Gonzalez listened attentively. Palacios' friend and now brother-in-law cracked his knuckles and stared outside. Without turning into the room, he responded, "ETA's a possibility, Toni. But they usually give a warning, and this time none was received. And they have not claimed responsibility yet. The elections are close but not imminent. And so many deaths! Until last night the most devastating ETA attack was the 1987 Barcelona parking lot bombing. Twenty-one people died, twenty one were left disabled. If this is ETA, it's new and confusing. You'll recall that the bombing at Atocha train station in Madrid was caused by radical Islamists. That attack killed 194 people." Gonzalez turned to face Toni and rubbed his forehead where a remnant of a street fight slashed through his eyebrow up to his hairline. Toni knew that the scar dated back to Javier's college days, when a would-be robber's knife sliced him right above the eye. In the end, Javier broke both the attacker's arms. God, he's a tough motherfucker, thought Toni.

Palacios and Gonzalez had been friends for more than twenty years when they became roommates at the university, sharing a mutual patriotism and interest in Spanish history and law enforcement. They established the first university group studying Spanish politics and current criminal events. Gonzalez knew his stuff.

"If ETA is not behind this, then who?" asked Toni.

"I don't know," responded Javier. "But if we see another incident in a brief period of time, at the very least we need to consider other terrorist groups, since ETA has single attacks only."

The two men stood facing each other, Toni at six feet eight inches tall with a sleek build was looking down at his six-foot brother-in-law. They'd been through a lot together. Ever since Jav saved his ass during a bodega row, they had been like brothers. One night, after sharing several bottles of rioja, the friends were caught off guard. Two local men from a group of six compadres tried to take on Toni. Blindsiding him from behind, they knocked him to the ground with punches to the ribs, then the abdomen and jaw. Within seconds Javier attacked one then the other, and in less than a minute both lay unconscious on the floor. Toni remembered rising to full height to ask the other four if they still harbored any complaints. The memory brought a smile to Toni's face.

"Why the grin?"

"Oh, nothing. Was thinking about that brawl when you laid those two guys out in thirty seconds flat." Javier still had a barrel chest, muscular neck and powerful 220-pound body.

"One of our finer moments. My sister made it clear that we're not to engage in any more barroom brawling. Got it?" joked Gonzalez. "Now look, what ETA wants most is respect and sovereignty, a goal common to many of us Basques. They are extremely proud of their culture, their history, and above all their language. But they also want amnesty for all imprisoned members, even if they have been convicted of murder, kidnapping, or conspiracy. Their targets usually consisted of police personnel, prison leadership, city officials, judges, or university professors who publicly disagreed with them. I think we just keep an open mind about the perpetrators at this early phase of the investigation."

Toni nodded. "I'm aware that our economy is tanking and an angry citizen might take out his anger and frustration in a form of terror, Javier."

"True. And the terrorist activity in Paris by radicalized French Islamists is a reminder of the sense of disenfranchisement some feel and their explosive response." Toni repeated his mantra: "Never let your guard down, even when things look calm, especially when things look calm."

The phone on Toni's desk rang. His assistant relayed that a secure call from London was on hold. Toni waited for the transfer and answered simply, "Palacios."

"Hello, Captain Palacios. Elizabeth Foster. MI-5."

Toni had never worked with Elizabeth Foster but knew her by reputation: tough-minded, careful, athletic, and beautiful. He'd also heard that a prize catch had eluded her in London a few years before. Something related to a near miss, an aborted biological terror incident. She had admitted her mistakes, remained at MI-5, and continued to build a portfolio of subsequent successes. He respected this woman.

"Please call me Toni. May I place you on speaker with Commander Javier Gonzales?"

"Sure. I've updated myself about your train station bombing and wanted to alert you to something else. Two physician friends of mine coincidentally are on holiday in Barcelona with families. Both of them worked with me in the pursuit of bioterrorists in London a few years ago. I received a call from one of them who told me that both men thought that on a nearby beach they had sighted a person of deep interest to me and MI-5."

She explained that one of the physicians had been careful to secure a water glass touched by the person of interest, the young woman at the beachside bar, who was possibly Diana Kontos. She reviewed their roles in the London bioterror event and their possible sighting of Kontos, acknowledging their likely overreaction to any terrorist incident in Europe and the good possibility of mistaken identity on their part.

"One of the physicians was briefly taken hostage as part of a robbery scam unrelated to the terror incident in London. He was petrified by the incident. I really think that he has a propensity for seeing the ghosts of the terrorists."

Elizabeth mentioned a very up-to-date official sighting of Kontos, confirming her recent presence in Morocco, a brief sea trip away from Spain.

"I am waiting to confirm the fingerprints on the glass as Diana Kontos's, and if so, I'd like to join forces with you. I've expedited the fingerprint identification process." She had already arranged for the forensic team to stay in the laboratory for a special testing of materials; the results would hopefully arrive by 8:00 p.m.

"We would welcome you warmly, Elizabeth, if you decide to travel here. You may have much-needed insights for us. We were just discussing the broad spectrum of likely operatives here. Just let us know the results of the study and of your plans. In the meantime, if any of our ongoing surveillance and intelligence activities points to your person of interest, I'll notify you immediately. In addition, I will make sure that you have access to all surveillance data of interest. Just call this number and ask for our director of surveillance activities."

"Thanks, Toni. I will add that I have rung up several colleagues in an attempt to get updates on the surveillance of Diana Kontos. No new leads from the Middle East or Europe. I will contact my colleagues in Egypt to check on any sightings."

Toni called an immediate staff meeting and reviewed the conversation with his colleagues. He reported that all tests showed no weapons of mass destruction and that the physical damage was caused by common explosive materials.

Four hours later a second call to Toni from Elizabeth was alarming. "Our agent in Marrakesh just confirmed a positive sighting in Casablanca six days ago. They were tracking Diana Kontos and thought she was holed up in one of the small hotels. However, just today they learned that she left two days earlier. No one knows her next destination. Unfortunately, we received a call from the Lyon headquarters that one of our colleagues from Interpol is missing – she completely vanished, and we fear the worst."

# XI

J oaquin Lopez thirsted for Spain's return to international influence and prosperity. Placing the urgency of the forthcoming meeting into historical perspective for his advisory board, he noted, "Each conquest was accompanied by transient periods of flourishing before another intrusion. The vast cultural diversity of national artifacts surely attests to Spain's sustained resilience. Thank you, ladies and gentlemen, for your time this morning. The president and I value your efforts and understand your commitment to the project and tactics under way." Joaquin Lopez, the aide to Spain's prime minister, addressed the 15 people gathered in the ministry's library around the oblong mahogany table sitting below a huge crystal chandelier. Most of the audience were experienced leaders in security, communication, and logistics. Each felt the weight of their duties in the context of the recent bombing.

"As I left my home this morning, my ten-year-old twin girls told me that my gray suit made me look very old, and my wife said my tie with abstract art made me look childish. I hope to strike a better balance with your responses today." The audience brightened and briefly chuckled; Joaquin wished he could stay on these softer subjects.

"We have only two more days before the prime ministers of the U.K. and France join a unique meeting with their counterparts from China and Russia. The secretary of state for the United States has confirmed that she also will be joining us. Early reports are optimistic that all are on board, but don't take anything for granted. Your attention to detail will be critical and may forge a new effort for reducing tensions in the Middle East. This may be the last chance we have to help create a two-state solution for Israel and Palestine. My goal, the country's goal, is to provide a productive meeting offering comfort for our guests. However, safety is our top priority.

"These are high stress times, ladies and gentleman." Joaquin continued. "The president of France is up for re-election, and a successful outcome here will give him huge political currency in a heated race with his opponents from the radical right wing party. Recent terrorist events have been stressful for his administration. The Russian prime minister hopes to recoup some international standing that was eroded after his country occupied Crimea, threatened Ukraine, assisted in the downing of Malaysia's commercial airliner, and continued to back Syria during the rebellious challenges to Assad and that country's brutal civil war. The financial crisis in the U.K. and recent sexual scandals involving the prime minister's cabinet have been damaging. He would like to draw the national media's attention away from these topics. Furthermore, the Chinese would love to extend their diplomatic and political influence both in Europe and the Middle East, hoping to further blunt the impact of the U.S. Lastly, it is clear the U.S. is fighting hard to remain number one in a world of increasing equals."

Lopez had prepared his words carefully and understood the many moving parts of the new realpolitik: America was in a state of decline in global influence and in the next 20 years risked being second to a rising China. India and Pakistan, both nuclear powers, were waging a surrogate war in Afghanistan. America wanted peace between Japan and North Korea and hoped to broker a better relationship between Japan and China for regional stability. An increasingly aggressive Russia harbored hope for the return of the Soviet Union level of global influence.

As for the Middle East, Lopez was convinced that the United States had squandered an opportunity after the fall of the Soviet Union in 1991. His mentor, Professor Zbigniew Brzezinski, from his public policy study at Harvard, had said as much. As the sole global leader, the U.S. could have moved quickly to create an independent Palestine state and could have begun to reduce the ongoing Arab-Israeli tension. Without a separate state, the Middle East would never be stable, and Israel would never achieve real peace. Israel might be both a victim of nuclear bombs or a premature deliverer of them, as Iran and other countries sought their own nuclear programs.

Peace in the Middle East was a key component of constraining Iran's nuclear ambitions and in keeping Israel from making premature military strikes. Establishing new trust was essential to broker a Palestinian state with the support of Israel. This could only happen if Iran backed off its current nuclear trajectory and Israel offered genuine concessions to the Palestinians.

"Spain's leadership role in helping contain Iran's nuclear ambitions is an incredible opportunity," said Lopez. At the briefing yesterday, the president had reminded them of the Arab uprisings that began in Tunisia in the spring of 2011 and spread like wildfire across northern Africa to the Middle East. The outpouring of citizens seeking democracy was encouraging but also served to heighten Israel's worries about a nuclear-armed Iran in the increasingly unstable area, especially with the departure of U.S. troops from Iraq. The president outlined Spain's key goal: to help constrain Iran, using diplomacy, and to see that country scale back its nuclear power ambitions. Israel had hinted strongly in unofficial communications that if Iran's ambitions were contained, talks of a Palestinian state could go forward. An important tactic was to elicit help from Russia, a critical ally of Iran. Lopez was also well aware of Spain's own challenges. New calls for a separate Catalonian state followed in the footsteps of Spain's rising unemployment. ETA's goals were uncertain at this point.

"If all multinational representatives coming to Barcelona agree on the new sanctions for Iran and also accept closer ties to Iran if they cooperate, then the risk of an Israeli preemptive move will be greatly reduced. We may even see a breakthrough in planning for a separate Palestinian state." Lopez also wanted Israel to dial back its rhetoric about a need to hit Iran if they appeared to continue to build nuclear capability. He outlined another goal to convince Israel that continued building of settlements in occupied Palestine was counterproductive, and that perhaps their war in Gaza with so many casualties was also harmful to their international reputation.

Dr. Isabel Becowitz, an undersecretary from Cuerpo National de Policia, raised her hand to offer dissent. "We and France have always been too soft on terrorists and have failed every time, so how can you blame Israel – always tough and consistent – for building settlements and bombing the hell out of the Palestinians?"

"That's simply untrue, Dr. Becowitz. We and our French colleagues have not failed to respond forcefully, killing many terrorists in the past," responded Lopez.

"Only when our own security is directly involved; we conveniently look the other way when it comes to terrorism in other countries. If we are not against all terrorists at all times, we are soft, and the terrorists win," said Becowitz, emotion rising in her voice.

"I see your point, though I might have phrased it differently. Consider Spain as committed to controlling terrorists," noted Lopez. "And that leads to my next point. The bombing here last night puts new pressure on us to increase security and show our resolve in dealing with what is most likely another ETA terrorist attack. ETA would love nothing more than to embarrass the government again. I am sure that's the end of it, but our allies and colleagues, who don't know ETA, will not be so assured."

Another hand rose, this time from Francisco Ponce de Leon, a leading anti-terrorist analyst. "But we have precious little evidence that this attack is ETA. I won't say you are naïve in your current opinion but would humbly suggest a more open-minded view until all the facts are in."

Lopez's face flushed. He had to agree.

"Agreed. So, let's summarize what we know so far: a train side bomb has killed twenty, including some American and British embassy staff members; over fifty others were wounded, twenty-two of them hospitalized, and four of the twenty-two are on life-support. Many patients who were detained briefly in emergency rooms or the hospital had no physical injury but apparently needed medical care. There is no evidence of radiation activity and no chemical or biological weapons. No warning was given, and no one has called to claim responsibility for the bombing." Lopez listed the facts deliberately, careful not to veer too far into editorial comments.

"Only a few minutes ago we learned that two Iranian tourists making anti-Israeli statements have been held as persons of interest and have neither denied nor confessed to being involved. Curiously, they have been implicated in the bombing of a synagogue in Greece, although we know nothing more at this time. They may be unreliable crazies with nothing to do with the explosions, or they may be critical to the incident.

"There are no leads suggesting a link to Al Qaeda or ISIS, but it is quite early. Currently we have an open mind. The consequences of terrorism in Barcelona at this time are considerable." He paused briefly to collect his thoughts and examine the expressions on his team members' faces.

"While we focus on terrorism, let's not forget the basics: protection of our visitors of state, attention to any of their health needs, and awareness of any food allergies or particular dislikes and preferences. Health and safety are our primary concern. For example, the prime minister of our own country has coronary artery disease requiring a cardiac device implanted in his chest wall to control his heart rhythm; the French prime minister is a brittle diabetic. These particular health issues are just as important to our team as ensuring physical security. We have a special medical and nutrition team working with our chefs."

Lopez reiterated the key goal of containing Iran. "If we fail, Spain will have failed to emerge as a serious political voice in Europe. It has occurred to us that a right wing extremist group or a deeply disturbed individual from our own country could be involved in the local bombing just as happened in Norway in 2011, the U.S. in 2012, and in both Paris and Copenhagen in 2015 and 2016. If we fail to apprehend such a person or persons, more deaths could be in the offing.

"Oh, and one more thing." Lopez paused to recognize both Dr. Becowitz and Señor Ponce de Leon. "If the terrorist act itself is eventually shown to represent a trial now of some sort to prepare for a more colossal event, ladies and gentlemen, we are in for one hell of a serious future. And we will respond appropriately. Now, let's go around the table to get updates and raise questions. I also want to know what might go wrong."

Three other people immediately raised their hands.

Mother of God, this is never easy, thought Lopez, betraying his concerns behind a wide smile.

# XII

In a café on Calle Gaude, Panos Trilla listened as Diana Kontos was explaining that if Israel could be distracted into a war with Iran, especially with a pre-emptive strike, it would cost them severely, economically and politically. She reasoned that they would even lose some close allies if they moved unilaterally. It would be the tipping point for distancing the U.S.-Israeli relationship which had shown some splintering in recent years because of the hugely disproportionate Palestinian death toll from the Israeli forces. Panos' daughter Kleïs, dressed as usual in men's clothing, sat next to Diana, resting her hand on Diana's thigh. A fractured U.S.-Israeli relationship would also take Israel's focus off Palestine so that she could continue her efforts not just for sovereign statehood, but also for revenge. Not just a directly personal revenge but an effort to pay for the pain her mother, uncles, and grandparents suffered when the Zionists settled in Israel in 1948, the killing of all of the men, the loss of their homes, the humiliation of her grandmother and mother living in a refugee camp with nothing to their name but the useless keys to a once-owned home.

"With your help, ETA can again be strong," responded Trilla, softly explaining that his friends were seeking autonomy and the overthrow of those who continue to deny them their independent heritage. They were a splinter group of the old ETA, more violent and less patient than the mother organization. "And my friends in Ajaccio look forward to ending France's control of Corsica," he added. "Both groups will support your focus in the Middle East. The world is about to change." His mind swelled with thoughts of Ajaccio.

Panos Trilla had grown up in Crete at a time when no one should have contracted smallpox. His mother was a waitress from Corsica, and his father a Catalonian engineer whose work providing clean water took him to the capital city Heraklion several times a year, where he rented a room above her restaurant on each visit. He had been charmed by the smile and beautiful legs of this kind woman whom he would eventually marry. Panos' parents' response to international requests for expertise in water purification during a cholera epidemic in East Pakistan led to the family's move in 1950 to what is now Bangladesh. It was there in Dakka that he was exposed to smallpox with no prior vaccination. His body quickly surrendered to the infection at the age of ten. He survived, but a severely pock marked face would be his reminder of a childhood era of careless attention to international health risks and to a family member's well-being.

He eventually blamed his parents for their thoughtless inattention to him. Moreover, he acquired a global perspective marked by anger at all large states for their neglect of the poor. A political science major at the University of Athens, Panos became a far left radical as a teenager, joining groups that opposed the military junta in Greece at the time. Eventually embracing the ideas of the National Liberation Front of Corsica, he accepted assignments on several occasions in bombings directed at

France, and was recognized as an expert in explosives including small units used by suicide bombers. Later he also developed a kinship with those Basque hardliners who still sought separation from Spain.

He knew that the new secret alliance of ETA with the National Liberation Front of Corsica would help both groups seek separation from the dominant countries of Spain and France. There needed to be some weakness created in the governments of Spain and France so that the negotiations could begin which would effect a free Basque country and a free Corsica. Success here would allow a major focus on the Middle East and especially on Israel.

Panos focused his eyes on his daughter and then on Diana, his daughter's companion, now so close. He loved Kleïs and had come to accept her sexual preference and transgender affectations, though he couldn't comprehend it at all. Out of extreme deference he would in public refer to Kleïs as *him*. But he could never completely abandon his feelings of Kleïs as his little girl. Life didn't always deliver the family you envisioned, but he was committed to being a supportive father, something that had been hollowed out of his own upbringing. He loved her intensely and would sacrifice his life for hers anytime. Only one time did he admit that he had fallen short of being a good parent to Kleïs and had failed to recognize something important happening in his own home. But he couldn't talk about it. It was his secret and Kleïs' as well. An older cousin spending the summer with Panos' family when Kleïs was only thirteen had abused her for weeks before being discovered. There were clues, but Panos missed them all. Shame and guilt were his constant companions.

"Should anything happen to the representatives of the key nations, our causes will be greatly advanced," said Panos soberly. "The meetings of heads of state or their representatives provide a once-in-a-lifetime opportunity. Our initial planning and apparent success went well. I want to stay focused on one of our pressing key issues, the movement of money from international sources sympathetic to Palestine and to the National Liberation Front of Corsica via Spain and to our special friends in the Middle East. And Kleïs, your talents are essential in our international efforts." He also recognized that if the next phase of the plan went well, an even larger plan could be developed with enormous consequences.

Kleïs had been able to utilize her proficient computer skills and social networking expertise to develop international support for Palestine in the last year. Panos followed her work closely and marveled proudly at her talents. She had devised an elaborate scheme for money laundering that included collaborators in Barcelona. She was planning important new projects, never previously accomplished. Kleïs turned to Diana and asked, "What about the American and English physicians we saw in the hotel lobby?"

"An unexpected surprise. A random holiday event," said Diana. "However, they remind me of bad luck. I had hoped to frighten them away with the phone calls. But if they do not leave, I will plan to immobilize them. They happen to be at the wrong place at the wrong time. I cannot forgive or forget anyone linked to the thwarting of our plans in London or the killing of my sister."

"Should we ask Ramón to neutralize them?" asked Kleïs.

"No, just distract or intimidate them. If something happens to them, it's possible that a link back to me may be considered. Right now no one knows I'm here in Spain. No one even knows that I have left Palestine. I just don't want the two vacationing physicians in the way. I'm not sure why, but I worry they may get involved."

"They don't even know that you're in Europe or even alive. Why not completely ignore them?"

Diana rose to kiss Kleïs on her cheek. "Please humor me, Kleïs. I was shocked to see the Americans in the hotel. It was like a bad omen. I am my own damn Oracle, and I see a dark future with them nearby."

Diana looked away as though recalling a past event. "Only one thing would make me think otherwise, if somehow they could bring their friend from MI-5 to Spain, the person I hold directly responsible for Sasha's death. Then I would consider myself to have unusually good fortunes, to have a new opportunity for revenge, an eye for an eye. I still miss my sister terribly." She closed her eyes briefly. Panos nodded respectfully.

"For now I'll arrange for a distraction," said Diana, sending a text message.

"Are you enlisting help?" asked Panos.

"Yes. Ramón. He will help us," said Diana.

A few minutes later Diana's phone buzzed. She read the text out loud: "I am tied up with work at Tio Pépe's and will be unable to join you. I will call tomorrow to see what else is needed. Please know, the American and British tourists are about to have the devil scared out of them. They'll be booking a quick return to an English-speaking country!"

Panos listened attentively with restraint and respect. He understood Diana's larger interest in hurting Israel and a personal wish to eliminate an MI-5 agent whose pursuit had led to the death of Sasha, Diana's twin sister. Her medical background and especially her medical talents gave her skills that might be useful in the near future. Corsica's secession from France would likely follow a successful Basque revolution. Not an Arab Spring but a Mediterranean Spring, he thought, smiling.

"We need to stay focused, not be distracted," emphasized Panos. "If the American and British physicians distract you, you need to manage and eliminate that distraction. But we're running against the clock. Do what is needed." He stood up to leave, kissed Kleïs on the cheek and hugged Diana before departing.

Kleïs had assured her father that her current experiment had gone well, that she had successfully navigated a pathway, a clandestine surprise that would make Homer proud. She had found a soft spot that would reverse the current asymmetry.

"The Greeks will again surprise the Trojans, Dad."

Kleïs moved behind the chair where Diana sat, placing both arms around her and thanking her for helping her dad's mission. She kissed the right side of her neck.

"You two make me proud," said Panos as he left. "Be especially cautious."

"Are you worried, Dad?"

"I always worry. And I don't want to see anything happen to either of you."

# XIII

That evening at the Columbo restaurant, the smell of saffron suffused the room. It whetted Jake's appetite. He was grateful that his family and Chris's were still on vacation and had been able to gather for a paella dinner. The four teens sat at their own table away from the adults. Jake caught a few errant phrases describing plans for university, boyfriends, girlfriends, music, and an occasional joke. They exchanged Facebook and Twitter accounts, vowing to stay connected after the holiday.

Jake was pleased when the waitress suggested a rioja. "This wine will marry with the food in the most delicious manner. Muy rico!"

He had seen no new events reported on CNN Europe, and the newscasters had been speaking as though the tragic bombing was a fading memory of months ago. Fourteen survivors remained hospitalized. Jake hoped and prayed it was isolated.

He couldn't help but notice that Brice and Jane had begun a flirtatious exchange.

It wasn't long before the teenage pair asked to go on a walk to the lobby and maybe out to the front of the hotel, ensuring their parents they would be careful, wouldn't go far and wouldn't be gone long.

Mary and Deb were still laughing about Chris and Jake's apparent ghost sighting when Jake's iPhone rang. Damn! He had forgotten to silence it before they sat down. He hesitated, then answered.

"Jake, Elizabeth here. I hope I'm not disturbing your vacation. I just received the report on the fingerprints. Not what you expected, since they do not belong to Diana Kontos. Sorry to tell you but it appears to be a case of mistaken identity."

Jake had mixed feelings about this news. He was relieved but actually disappointed not to see Elizabeth, not to share another adventure with her.

He whispered to Chris, Mary and Deb, "The prints were not Diana's."

All seemed relieved, especially Deb, who called out an enthusiastic "Yes!"

"Curiously, however," continued Elizabeth, "the fingerprints matched those of a new recruit to a violent Corsican separatist group. But I reiterate, not Diana Kontos. So you didn't see her after all, and that should be of some comfort to both of us."

"We've had covert operatives working in Ajaccio," continued Elizabeth, "several as waiters in key restaurants. They have gathered top-secret information and built up a repository of fingerprints as part of base line surveillance. We don't know much about this person yet, but I have asked my colleagues to fill me in on any known background, skill set, and travels.

"At this point I conclude that you didn't see Diana Kontos, but I don't want to miss the remote possibility that the person whose prints are on the glass is in Spain with leads to the recent bombing. I've alerted our national and international teams at MI-5 and MI-6, and I'll fly by private jet late tonight. I'm going to have my husband join me, and he can catch up with some of his legal colleagues nearby while I work. The other reason for my call is this: can we meet socially for breakfast before I get a briefing from local authorities about the bombing incident?"

Jake answered with renewed animation. "Sure! Will 7:00 a.m. work? I'll ask Chris to join us. We're staying at the Hotel Isabella on the edge of the city." He provided the address and room numbers.

"That is perfect, Jake. I'll meet you in the restaurant of your hotel and look forward to seeing you."

Catching Deb's sardonic frown, Jake answered flatly, "That works well."

Jake spent some time explaining the call, the fact that the fingerprints on the glass failed to match those of Diana Kontos, but were possibly those of another person of interest to MI-5. He announced that Elizabeth would like to meet with Chris and him. He emphasized that she was bringing her husband, who would not be joining them for breakfast.

Everyone seemed relieved by the news, decompressed from a state of high alert and vulnerability. "Strange how a series of coincidences can disturb your peace of mind," said Mary.

"Right," agreed Chris. "This calls for another glass to celebrate our friendship and good luck." He poured the ladies and Jake another splash of the Rioja before finishing it in his own glass. "Cheers!"

"Cheers," echoed Jake and Deb. Deb remained restrained. Jake knew it must be the news of an attractive woman from MI-5 visiting, even if only for breakfast, during family vacation in Spain. He felt sure he would be hearing about this later that night.

Jake and Chris went to look for Brice and Jane. Everyone needed to get some rest before the rapid train ride to Seville the next day to catch bullfighting. Jake reassured the group that with heightened security measures in place, the trains would be the safest mode of transportation possible.

After several minutes of searching, the two teens still had not been found in the lobby, on the sidewalk outside the hotel or in the bar. Jake and Chris walked slowly; an uneasy feeling grew in Jake's stomach. He called both Deb and Mary to see if Brice and Jane had arrived in the rooms. "No, they're not here," each answered anxiously.

Jake said he'd walk around the block to see if they were nearby. Chris would remain by the front desk. First, he went to the hotel gift shop to purchase some ibuprofen. He had the beginning of a headache.

While Jake was buying the pills, he was surprised to see a glass table covering Carrera jewelry pieces, the same designer he had surprised Deb with on their arrival to Spain. He made a quick purchase.

He returned to meet Chris at the front of the hotel and began to walk alone around the perimeter of the block. Still no Brice or Jane.

Turning on to the next road, Jake looked both ways and walked towards the main street on which the hotel lay. A woman with a sign reading *El Tarot* approached him, inquiring in English, "Who are you looking for, Señor? I can help."

Her statement rattled Jake, who coughed twice before responding. "My teenage son and a girlfriend of his are probably walking around the hotel Isabella. I just wanted to be sure they are safe."

"For only three euros I can answer you."

Feeling anxious and unsure if he was a victim of serendipity or a plot to ask for ransom, he presented her the money.

Calmly she held his hands, facing the palm sides up and smiled while moving her finger softly over the creases of each. "You are a good father and anxious, but all will end well. Your son is in some danger, but his will pass and you will find him tonight."

Continuing on to the far side of the hotel, Jake was accosted by a man completely dressed in silver, his face and hands painted silver. He was holding a great silver cross on his shoulders – the crucifixion. He blocked any passage on the sidewalk, held out his hand and asked, "Dinero por favor?"

In his furor to traverse the entire perimeter of the hotel, Jake pulled out a five-euro bill and said, "Here!" pushing by the panhandler.

The man in silver responded in English. "Gracias, you will have luck, Señor."

Jake thought to himself, I hope I don't need it.

Reaching the front of the hotel, he saw no signs of either missing child. Approaching the doorman, he inquired if he had noticed a teenage boy and girl in the last half-hour.

"Yes, Señor. They walked to the corner and entered a private taxi and were driven off."

# XIV

Brice sat up tall next to Jane in a back seat of a private taxi with tinted windows, soundproofing and a Plexiglas barrier between them and the front seat. A man drove with a woman at his side. Brice wondered if the two women dressed like hotel clerks, offering free CDs and downloads of great music, had intentionally lured them into the car. They had told Brice and Jane about a great dancing venue with beautiful Spanish and Latino music. Looking for adventure, they had taken the women up on their offer to get them there. Half a block from the hotel, the back door of the car stood open. The two smiling ladies gave them their gifts, pointed to the back seats, and ushered them inside. Pleased to have received the CDs, Brice and Jane entered the car. One of the smiling ladies slammed the door shut as the cab sped off.

Holding Jane's shaky hand, Brice asked in Spanish, "A donde vamos, Señor?" The man answered all questions in Spanish. "To a dance club where you will have a great time. It's only ten euros cover charge, and you will have good drinks and see and learn the salsa, meringue and tango. It will be a unique experience. It will take less than twenty minutes to arrive there."

Fifteen minutes later, they arrived at La Cantina de Bailar. Again two smiling ladies greeted the car, opened the door on the pavement side, and allowed the passengers to exit. Brice paid the taxi bill and thanked the driver and companion properly. The evening began to unfold just at the man had predicted. Brice felt relieved.

Having been escorted to a table for two on an elevated platform with 100 people surrounding a dance floor, Brice ordered two sangrias, and he and Jane began a night of dancing and flirting. There were small candles in green glass containers at each table; the light inside the cantina was low, with the exception of bright lights on the band: a drummer, a base guitarist, a pianist and guitarist. All musicians were women.

In between songs, the dancers, recognizing the two as likely young Brits, would stop, pull them onto the studio floor, and teach them the basic steps to various dances, the rumba, lambada, salsa, and the tango. Halfway into the second drink, Brice and Jane were holding hands and dancing closely together, arms wrapped around each other.

At eleven o'clock, Brice called for and paid the bill, and he and Jane planned to hail a cab to go back to the hotel. He wasn't ready to return but knew they were probably already in a little bit of trouble. Even in the city, Brice could see the stars glittering in the sky on this moonless evening. Leaving the Cantina, he suggested a brief walk before taking a taxi home. Jane was delighted and leaned her head toward Brice's as the two teens walked with arms around each other's waists, oblivious to music emanating from two nearby bars.

The streets included the occasional deserted building, especially as they moved from La Cantina. It seemed the local people were eying them with suspicion. Three blocks later, just about the time the teens considered returning in the direction of the Cantina, they found themselves in front of a curious corner shop, Tio Pépe's Tattoos. Neither teen had a tattoo; they entered mostly out of curiosity.

"Welcome, amigos," said a man in English. He introduced himself as José. "How can I help you"?

Brice responded in Spanish and said that he knew nothing about tattoos and wanted to speak to someone about the process and price. He added that he didn't want one tonight but might return. He and Jane might commemorate their holiday with a very small tattoo. He smiled at Jane and put his arm around her.

"Let me introduce you to my manager, Ramón. Unfortunately our tattoo artist, Tio Pépe, is away. He will be back tomorrow afternoon."

A few moments later Ramón described the process, explaining the efforts used to insure safety and comfort. He offered them a special low price if they returned. He even gave them a brochure with examples of small tattoos that people in love had accepted and placed where their parents would not easily observe them.

Jane looked at Brice throughout the exchange, but once she looked at Ramón she quickly latched on to Brice's arm, her face chalked with sudden fear. She could barely get over the man's completely purple eyes, a sight that she had never seen before and that somehow made her uncontrollably nervous. She immediately looked away. For his part Brice was equally anxious but wanted to show control over the situation. After ten minutes, Brice thanked Ramón for his time and said that they would think about it. He grasped Jane's hand, and the two marched quickly to hail a cab on Calle de Luz.

"You made me feel safe in there, Brice. I was incredibly scared when I saw his eyes! I've never seen anything like that before."

One half-block from Tio Pépe's the two were startled when a man came out of an alley by an abandoned building. Holding a knife and speaking Spanish, he said, "Good evening, children. Now give me your money!"

Brice pulled out twenty euros, the only money he had left, all of which was in coins. As he held the change out in his hand, the man with the knife disregarded the coins, removed Brice's watch and disappeared back into the dark alley.

"Oh, my God. What a night," said Brice who spotted a taxi coming in their direction. He grabbed Jane's hand and both ran ahead, grateful that he had money for the taxi.

For the next twenty minutes they held each other's hands in the back seat. They made a pact that neither would discuss the visit to the tattoo shop or the robbery.

Chris and Jake were speaking to local enforcement officers in front of the hotel when Brice and Jane arrived. Mary and Deb remained in their respective rooms awaiting any possible phone call from the children.

As they left the taxi, the young couple exchanged glances. "It was great," Brice told Jane, squeezing her hand. He was elated to have had the night's adventure away from the family with a wonderful and pretty girl.

"I had a great time," whispered Jane. "What an adventure. Thank you, Brice." She squeezed his hand.

"You two scared the hell out of us," said Jake, whose fear had yielded to anger. "Where were you, what have you been up to?" Chris nodded but was relieved. He placed his arm around Jane and walked away.

"But, Dad, I am sixteen," said Brice. He decided not to discuss the loss of his watch.

"Don't you realize that you're in a town you don't know, in a culture where the danger signals are unknown to you? I want you to be more thoughtful, for Christ's sake!" Jake pointed to the elevators. They would have a longer heart-to-heart talk in the morning when the time was auspicious. He didn't like his son taking risks with a good friend's daughter in a town recently experiencing terror. Deb would surely blame him for Brice's careless indiscretions.

# XV

Diana was restless in bed next to Kleïs, questioning if she was excessively concerned about the two foreign physicians who were in Spain. Kleïs told her to stay focused on the mission, to stay motivated.

Diana became livid and immediately defended herself: "Motivation – my whole life is motivation! Motivation is in my DNA! I have no choice."

Kleïs apologized profusely, hugging Diana and cradling her head. She repeated sweet lines from Sappho until Diana fell into a very deep sleep.

Hours later, however, Diana was in a semi-awake state, caught somewhere between dreams and acute awareness of her hurt and anger. She was curious but not fearful of these visual experiences, even though these dreams made no sense. It seemed that space, time, physics, and logic had conspired to abandon her. Nocturnal fantasies had happened to her before on numerous occasions. She saw herself at age eleven in a refugee camp, in a room with cots from one wall to another, spaced only two feet apart. She recalled family members, friends, and strangers in the crowded room, and that night she felt blood in her vagina for the first time, lying on a cot with her mother and grandmother nearby. She was also in the company of several curious teenage boys two cots away, whom she tried to hide from under the thick blanket provided to her. She felt they tried to see her undressing. Would they see the blood against her pale green pajamas?

Even now, she could smell the acrid burning kerosene lamps that provided dim light in the room at night and neutralized the odor emanating from of the single bathroom in the building. Still locked in her dream state, she looked into a small pocketbook mirror, sometimes seeing her own face but also the face of her mother, then her grandmother and then back again to her own reflection. Strangely she took pleasure in observing the countenances of all three family members in the mirror, and embraced each with unconditional love. Yet she longed to speak; she had so many things she wished she could say to her mother and grandmother.

Tears began to flow from her eyes; they also slid down the face of her grandmother and mother. Now a vast waterfall formed and splashed on to a road below, surrounding the recently abandoned house of her grandparents in Palestine. To the pleasure of all her family members, the great torrent protected the family home like a moat, preventing anyone from approaching it to loot or vandalize.

Just then, the grinning teenage boys pointed to Diana but addressed her by the name of her mother. Of course they were addressing her mother, now awash in shame. Diana felt the weight of the filial embarrassment, the deep humiliation of internment after days of walking from Palestine, her grandmother continually holding only the keys to the now padlocked house, the useless keys, the symbol of the loss of her family's home, taken by the Zionists.

Anger warmed the back of her neck as she heard her mother calling to her grandmother to take her away from the prison, the refugee camp.

Where were her uncles, her father? Her grandmother did not tell her that the men had been taken away at gunpoint, shackled tightly in trucks, never to return – the victims of the new authority of Israel.

Diana, her grandmother, and mother were now interchangeable, three faces with the same body standing next to each other, with hollow expressions and mouths open wide as though incredulous of fate's cruel betrayal.

Diana floated above the people, above the houses. She willed this ascension, defying the vigilant pull of gravity, mind and body free of strife, and imagining a life with opportunity. The remarkable transition from hopelessness was accompanied by an indelible drive to avenge.

The dream took her to a couch, where she sat next to her twin sister, Sasha. They were children in a small house outside of Athens, listening to their mother describe the hatred that she and their grandmother held for the Israelis. They told her that she needed to right the wrongs imposed on the Palestinians by the invaders from Europe, the same people who had escaped their own threat of extinction in the early 1940s. Her mother repeated the call for retaliation, payment for what was due, a restoration of justice. She then pointed to a ceramic statue on the table, a gray figure of the goddess Themis, overseer not of human or popular justice but of a divine law, the will of the gods. Her grandmother told the girls she would read them the story as told by Homer later that day.

Diana's father then appeared in the living room, a young handsome man telling the girls that he needed to be away to continue to help his people fight repression. He apologized and said he would discuss more when they were older. He then picked up a small travel bag and left. Her mother proudly spoke to the girls of their father's bravery, extolling his dedication to justice, the enemy of intolerance.

The scene changed, and Diana and Sasha were together, young teens in bed at home, vowing to hand out retribution when they were older, to restore the family honor, to create safe harbors for the Palestinians. They were lying next to each other, holding hands, talking quietly about a future when they and their mother would return to Palestine and walk proudly through the streets of the original village. Father would be home every night for dinner; the people who had humiliated Diana's family members would have been driven away in ignominy.

Next, Diana appeared as a student in a classroom learning *The Iliad* in Greece, reading about Chimera, with the head of a lion breathing on its enemies, the head of a goat with a *terrible flame of bright fire* perched above its back, and a snake at the end of its tail. Homer had willed the anger of Chimera on the enemies of freedom. The Greek culture had many guardians of truth, of fairness to watch over its people. She would commit to memory the stories of the war in Troy.

Still carried by her subconscious, Diana traveled to her life in her forties, in bed again but this time with her lover Jeffrey, a caring man, a surgeon who always made her feel special. He could take her to an emotionally safe haven, one without hate. He was a good man and gentle lover, who should never have died. And it was such a terrible death caused by accidental transmission of the designer *Staph aureus* strain of bacteria, the guilt would never leave Diana. The unseen pathogens had hidden under her fingernails and had entered the skin of the man she loved. She wept in the dream – for him and for herself, carrying a burden never to be lifted. Even with such risk, she was already preparing another engineered organism, which would infect, paralyze, and kill Israelis and Israeli sympathizers in London. She and Sasha had combined their talents of molecular biology and toxicology to design the perfect pathogen with genes coding antibiotic resistance, aggressiveness, and paralysis of all muscles with botulism toxin all at once.

Suddenly Diana was fearful in a car racing from the pursuant MI-5 and police in London; the car crashed, and Diana could feel nothing but pain. The dream was now a nightmare. Looking across the front seat, she saw Sasha sat motionless, her eyes open and blank. She left the world suddenly, prematurely. Diana lay still in a hospital bed, pinned down by pain in every limb. Putting on the garb of an aging Greek nun, she hobbled past the armed guard while her youthful accomplice, who had entered the hospital disguised as an old religious sister with special agility, escaped through the hospital window.

Still adrift in her mind's epic narrative, she traveled to a Palestinian hospital, where her son cried out his first breath upon entering the world, and Diana felt no pain, only joy. She named the boy Achilles, holding him to her breasts, telling him he would be the best and bravest above all others. "You are my hero and will be the hero of all our people burdened with so much grief inflicted by others." She kissed his forehead. She saw him again on his first birthday crawling around the living room of his aunt, his full time nanny. The boy held his arms up to Diana.

A soft table light went on, and Diana felt the gentle hug of Kleïs next to her. Stretching her arms slowly, Diana recounted the features of her dream to Kleïs, who listened attentively. Awakened from her past, Diana rested in the embrace of this woman.

"Your dreams are a favorable omen, Diana, and I am glad you are with me, my love. I want our project to succeed more than you could ever imagine."

She whispered into Diana's ear:

*Voices…loved…of those who have died…speak to us in dreams … and for a moment return sounds from our life's first poetry – like music at night, distant, fading away."*

"Thank you, Kleïs, I love Cavafy, and I love you."

Kleïs picked up Diana's hands, turned her palms up and kissed each, then held them on each side of her face.

"Thank you, Kleïs. I want to place my memories aside, remove all barriers between us," she said, gently tugging on the ties of Kleïs pajamas to expose the beautiful triangle of soft hair above parted thighs.

# XVI

Jake and Brice opened the door to the hotel room. Deb jumped up from the bed and hugged Brice tightly, telling him how relieved she was that he and Jane were safe. She confessed that she had imagined the worst scenario: they were kidnapped or injured or worse. Brice shrugged it off with a "Sorry, Mom."

"You better get a good night's rest," she instructed, still visibly shaken. Brice reassured her he would and headed to his adjoining room. The door latched, and Deb turned to face Jake. Somehow, he knew she was irritated about something more than Brice.

"And you tell me that you're having breakfast with Elizabeth Foster tomorrow?" She seethed, clearly incredulous at the prospect. "You mean to tell me that that woman from MI-5 is coming into our life again? You're not a terrorist detective; you're a doctor! And a father and a husband! If we are in danger, we need to consider leaving early. If this has nothing to do with Diana Kontos, why is Elizabeth Foster coming to Barcelona to see you? I don't like it one bit."

Jake did his best to explain that this was a brief social breakfast, that Chris would be joining as well and that Elizabeth's husband was coming to Barcelona. Jake mentioned that the fingerprints were from a person of interest to MI-5, even if not Diana Kontos. Elizabeth wanted to thank him for the clue.

Deb turned away with a scowl and prepared to go to bed. Jake turned on the television, but found only sports updates. He slowly got ready for bed; Deb had already crawled under the covers and was lying at the far edge of the bed with her head facing the wall. Deb was mad. But he couldn't stop thinking about seeing the woman he occasionally fantasized about. Deb lay quietly. He hoped she would sleep and not stew about Elizabeth Foster. Jake couldn't sleep. He was too excited about seeing Elizabeth the next morning. He closed his eyes.

At 7 a.m., Elizabeth Foster walked into the cafe in a white suit; her skirt fell just above her knees. Jake thought that one rush of air might lift the lightweight material like a silk kite. He took in her bright smile, high cheekbones, and swept-back chestnut hair and immediately wrapped his arms around her. He inhaled the scent of her perfume, his face grazing her neck and then kissed her cheek.

"Good morning, Elizabeth. You look wonderful." He scanned her face, her mouth, her narrow waist, long legs, and the soft bulge of her breasts. The magical moments they experienced in London drifted through his head.

"Good morning, my friend." She hugged Jake, pressing her hands on his back for a few seconds.

"Thank you for meeting with me on your holiday. I hope you don't mind my asking for a private alcove down the corridor so that we can speak freely."

"Not at all," said Jake, delighted to be alone with the woman he had longed to see. "Unfortunately, Chris received a call from his lab in Oxford this morning and has to miss you. They're having a quality control problem; one of the new tests requires his perspective."

"I understand. I doubt that I'll be long in Barcelona, but I thought that I should touch base with some local authorities about another person of interest who is apparently in Spain, the lead from you. And, of course, I did want to see you. But first, let's discuss business.

"I doubt that Diana has any role here, Jake, but she has left Palestine for North Africa, and we lost surveillance of her in Morocco. We're still looking for an Interpol colleague who vanished after spotting Diana in Casablanca. That intelligence, along with the prints of a person of interest from Corsica, gave me an incentive to visit. Well, that and an opportunity to catch up with you."

The waitress delivered juice and coffee and said she would return in a few moments to take breakfast orders.

"I've not learned anything insightful about the railroad bombing. Of some interest, however, I tapped into databases from sentinel hospitals here, a surveillance system of certain disorders, especially respiratory disorders. It was set up after your anthrax attacks in the U.S., designed to detect sudden increases in respiratory distress and pneumonias in order to screen for bioterror. But they collect information on any increase in clinic or hospitalizations rates.

"Since the explosion here, inpatient admissions are up significantly in our ten survey hospitals. These are not the injured patients. I'm not sure what it means. But I wondered if you'd be willing to look at the information. You'll have all data for the month before the incident and from the days since the incident. See, I'm trying to impress you! You taught me the importance of control groups when looking for clues to a new finding! I took the liberty of downloading the information." She slid a thumb drive across the table in his direction.

He was flattered. "No problem, Elizabeth. I'll gladly take a look. Do you have anything in particular you're looking for?"

"Not at all, Jake. I just thought you might notice something unusual, something medical that might be linked to the explosion. No evidence of weapons of mass destruction was found, so I'm at a loss. Perhaps this is just a random finding, and I'm just fishing."

The waitress appeared and asked if they had had enough time to consider the menu. Elizabeth settled for a frittata, and Jake asked for scrambled eggs and bacon. A few waiters at the edge of the restaurant seemed to take interest in them, the couple flirting over breakfast.

In between lingering looks, Elizabeth said that she had several formal visits planned with authorities and would keep Jake and Chris informed of any new information. If nothing of interest surfaced, she and her husband would order in at the hotel room or find a good Spanish restaurant for dinner.

"Jake, it's hard to believe that it's been two years." She grasped his hands.

"I agree. Time has slipped by quickly. I've missed you." Jake held her gaze, her softening smile. "I have a gift for you," he said, presenting Elizabeth with a box containing a gold necklace.

Elizabeth opened the gift, saw the necklace and held it up to her neck. "Jake, it's lovely! And so special. I cannot accept it, though. I thank you for your thoughts, but it is too much."

"Elizabeth," choked Jake, "This was not expensive, but I thought of you when I saw it. Please do accept it." Elizabeth said nothing.

"I hope it doesn't seem presumptuous or inappropriate, but when I knew you were coming, I wanted to mark the occasion. Perhaps you'll think of me when you wear it."

Looking at Jake, she said softly, "OK and thank you" and placed it around her neck.

Jake was relieved. "How are you doing in general?"

"On a personal note, my boys are doing well scholastically and also on the football pitch. My husband is not completely well, but I don't think I can talk about that."

"Of course, no problem, Elizabeth."

"I've missed you terribly, Jake, personally and even our mutual quest of a bioterrorist," she quipped with a broad smile. "I hope you haven't discovered another woman in law enforcement to help you track down criminals?"

Jake shook his head – no – to this oblique inquiry. The only "other" woman was his wife.

"How is your family, Jake?"

"We're fine, thanks. Brice and Tracy are here with us and excited to be in Spain. They're good kids. I'm grateful."

"Is your wife happy to be on holiday here in Spain?"

"I think she is. She especially seems to be enjoying catching up with Chris's wife, Mary. They've been close friends since my sabbatical in London twelve years ago." He squirmed to avoid any comment about the recent discord related to Elizabeth's being in Barcelona.

"Does your wife like travelling with you?"

"She's selective. No overnighters. No trips where she'll be alone all day while I speak or am tied up with colleagues. She says she can be at home alone and get things done."

"Is she still working?"

"Yes, full time. Things are a bit hectic at home, and I continue to be busy at the hospital."

"Does she mind your heavy commitment to medicine and the world's infectious diseases?"

"Most of the time, she's tolerant of my time away from home, but she has an occasional objection. At the same time she is proud of what I do. Sometimes I think she wishes she had more time with me."

"That's good, Jake!" She seemed to like his responses. "May I call you if I find some free time here?"

"Absolutely."

"Wonderful, Jake." She squeezed his hands. "Maybe we could share some wine here, a good port to recall our time in London. I wish we could linger here. I have to meet Commander Javier Gonzalez in 30 minutes. I'll stay in touch and will sincerely look for opportunities to meet while we're both in Barcelona. You are so sweet to meet me on your holiday, Jake. And thank you for the necklace. It will remind me of you."

"I wouldn't have missed this. You know that, I think."

Elizabeth smiled, "Perhaps our paths will cross soon. In the meantime, please let me know if any of the hospital admissions data raises eyebrows, clinically speaking."

"I'll try to have something for you tonight, Elizabeth." The desire to find a few hours alone with Elizabeth surfaced from deep within. He had lied to Deb and hadn't been completely honest with himself this morning. There was no denying that he wanted this woman. As both stood up, Jake gave her a firm hug; his hands slid down the small of her back and skimmed her buttocks for a moment.

"Thank you, Jake." She kissed his lips pressing both hands softly on either side of his head and turned to leave. Jake felt young again, tracing the graceful movement of her long athletic legs pacing down the hallway, her delicate skirt rhythmically swaying side to side.

# XVII

E scorting agent Foster to a bright conference room, Toni Palacios admired her athletic appearance and height of almost six feet. She *is* beautiful, he thought. In the center of the room was a rectangular white pine table surrounded by six chairs with red seat cushions. "Por favor," he said, inviting her to sit down.

Her strong gaze impressed him. He had the sense she could look right through him, read his mind. She probably knows I find her attractive, he thought. She's polite and full of confidence and doesn't seem to be deferential to men of great height. If I were a criminal, I would not want her tracking me down.

"Agent Foster, may I introduce my colleague, Javier Gonzalez." Both men took seats directly across the table from Elizabeth.

"Thank you, Toni. Delighted to meet you, Javier. I know of you both from the Madrid train bombing case; Director Casewell speaks highly of your work. Thank you for taking time with me this morning."

"Equalmente. We are honored to meet you, as well," said Javier, "We followed the bioterror case, of course. Great work in London."

"As I mentioned to you on the phone, two skilled physician friends of mine who were instrumental in thwarting the bioterrorists in London happen to be on holiday here. One is a professor of microbiology at Oxford with IT oversight and expertise in molecular biology and genetics. His friend is an American professor of infectious diseases from Stanford University with expertise in epidemiology. On the nearby Nova Icaria beach they happened to notice a person who looked like – remarkably similar to – the mastermind of the London terror event. We at MI-5 had tracked her to Palestine but learned that she was recently in Morocco. We had a lead there in Casablanca, but our intelligence source went silent. We fear that she was identified and possibly eliminated. Thus, I remain quite concerned that our person of interest may have returned to Europe.

"To their credit and with great ingenuity and curiosity, my friends gathered up a glass touched by this person. They wrapped it in a serviette to avoid touching it and express-mailed it to me. I had our lab dust it for prints. It turned out to be someone else's prints, those of a person who has attended meetings of terrorist groups in Corsica.

"It seems to be a strange coincidence, Toni, but my curiosity drives me here. We, of course, would like to know more about a terrorist from Corsica and why that person is here and who is accompanying that person. In addition, you have had a serious terrorist incident at a nearby train station. I wonder if any of this is related. I realize that I may be trying to apply Occam's razor to a series of highly unrelated events, but it seems prudent to check it out.

"In summary, my physician friends saw a person of interest, a woman whom they believed to be the mastermind of the London bioterror activity, the one who escaped to Palestine. They gathered a glass that she touched, but the prints match those of a person linked to a terrorist cell in

Corsica. We know little about that person at this time. Do you think any of this may relate to groups who might have set off explosions here?"

"The impulse here, Elizabeth," said Toni, "is to blame ETA. However, some pieces don't fit their usual pattern. For example, there was no warning, and no acknowledgement after so many deaths. In the middle of the night, we booked two Iranians on our watch list who confessed to the killings, but we cannot tie them to the bombing site when the explosion occurred.

"The motivation for their confession is unclear, especially since a key goal of the international meeting is to seek concessions from Iran in not building a nuclear weapon.

"So your thoughts about other terrorist groups involved in our incident would be extremely interesting. We have an open mind at this time. Javier and I agree that with any new incident we must consider a broad array of terrorist groups, including homegrown, disaffected individuals. The killings in Paris in early 2015 have us on edge.

"Our agents are interviewing anyone linked to prior terror events whether in jail or in the community and are even speaking with family members and reviewing their travel schedules, hard drives, texts, and calls. Those with recent trips to the Middle East are especially suspect. With help from intelligence we're monitoring all communications of high-risk people, monitoring social media and underground websites. It's a new world," said Javier.

"We've found absolutely no trace of biological, nuclear or chemical weapons of mass destruction. Specifically, no people exposed to the explosion have elicited symptoms suggesting these issues.

"Our question here in Barcelona is what was the goal of the terrorist incident, if not from ETA? We ask this especially in light of the very high-profile international meeting of heads of state. This has caused us great concern, and we feel as though we're waiting for the next shoe to drop, but we don't know when or what that will look like."

"As for the prints you identified, I suppose that the second person at the beach could have been an accomplice in terror," said Toni.

"Or your physician friend possibly chose the wrong glass," injected Javier, "and found this other person of interest by mistake."

"Either explanation is reasonable," said Elizabeth, "but it is odd and still of concern that someone of interest looked so much like our London bioterrorist.

"There is also another puzzle, gentlemen. Before leaving London, I learned that there was a spike in hospital admissions here beyond those injured in the bombing, perhaps not surprising in light of people's responses to terror. I may be on a heightened alert due to the bioterror we experienced in London a few years ago, but do you imagine that there is something more? In other words, are you sure that no strange substance was present?"

"A fair question, Elizabeth, but so far our experts say they can find nothing unusual."

"Thanks to you, one of your colleagues in Public Health gave me access to the ongoing surveillance database you have here. I apologize for not contacting you earlier about this. As I mentioned, one of the two doctors here, the one from Stanford, is a renowned epidemiologist, and I took the liberty of asking him to look at the data on hospital admissions. I hope you don't mind, and of course I will share any findings with you immediately."

"On the contrary, Elizabeth. Any insights will be greatly appreciated," Toni said.

"Thank you, gentlemen. I'll keep in contact and let you know anything I learn. I appreciate your time this morning," said Elizabeth, standing.

"What are your plans while you are here, Elizabeth? Will you need help arranging a hotel or suggestions for good restaurants?" asked Javier. "I am an expert on restaurants serving authentic regional cuisine and not so bad at recommending wine."

"Thank you, Javier. My husband is a barrister and is travelling with me. Tonight we may relax, and eat in our room at the hotel. Tomorrow, however, after he visits a few friends, Ian has tentatively planned a dinner at one of your famous seafood restaurants, La Santa Maria. I'll plan to leave either late tomorrow night or the following day if all leads are negative."

"La Santa Maria is excellent, Elizabeth, and one of my favorites. If you change your mind, my wife and I would be honored to give you a brief tour of our wonderful city and have you as our dinner guests at our home; perhaps Toni and his wife could join us." Elizabeth nodded appreciatively.

A harsh knock on the door alarmed all three; a red-faced man opened the door and quickly passed a note to Toni Palacios, apologizing to Elizabeth for the interruption.

"Javier, the second shoe may have dropped." Toni's face went ashen. "A small explosive has just gone off in a square outside a boutique hotel on the edge of town, the Hotel Isabella."

# XVIII

J ake and Deb sat across the aisle from Mary and Chris on the AVE, the rapid train from Barcelona to Sevilla, on their way to see a traditional bullfight, still legal in the old Roman town that hadn't changed much in 300 years. The four kids sat facing forward two aisles away, occupying the entire row. The dusty Spanish countryside raced by at over 250 kilometers per hour. The trip south would take over four hours with a brief stop in Madrid. Jake thought that a night in Sevilla would be refreshing, with a return the next day to Barcelona.

Jake observed flickering lines of data as he scrolled down a document on his laptop. He programmed the database to look for any differences in the uninjured patients who had been hospitalized just after the bombing versus those hospitalized in the weeks before. He wasn't sure what he might find, perhaps a difference in age or gender, underlying disorders, acute versus elective admissions, surgical versus medical patients, perhaps more psychiatric patients disproportionately susceptible to the fears that surround a terrorist event.

Deb read a brochure about Sevilla provided by AVE, still visibly annoyed at Jake. She had been chilly all morning and told him that she was pissed. He continued to be engrossed with the police work of a British spy agent and not with his wife and children. Her last words before they left their hotel room were, "Get your head out your work, Jake. After all this is a family vacation, a fucking *family* vacation!"

Despite Deb's anger, Jake couldn't pull himself away from the data. His first · pass showed that a somewhat higher percentage of *recently* hospitalized patients were older men who had either suffered heart failure or were diabetic, compared to the earlier pre-bomb period. The next step was to see if this trend lay within random variations or was a truly significant difference. He applied statistics.

Reprogramming the database to add rigorous statistical testing, Jake proceeded to the next step and discovered they were all significant. He looked at the relative odds – at least three-fold with each of the four variables. He then looked at the probability that the differences observed could be ascribed to chance alone, and it was tiny, less than one percent. In fact, his stats showed a probability value of less than 0.01!

He recalled his statistics professor at the London School of Hygiene and Public Health, Peter Smith. Prof had said that if you look at "causes" of cirrhosis, both smoking and alcohol showed up in the initial or univariate analysis, looking at one variable at a time. However, in multivariable analyses, after you corrected for the effect of alcohol, smoking was no longer important. The heavy users of alcohol were also likely to be smokers. So the true cause as shown in the more advanced analysis was likely alcohol, not smoking. In this case, smoking was a *confounder*, linked to the real cause and needing to be managed within the data in order to focus on the true predictor: alcohol.

Jake asked himself the key question with the current data: which was the most important difference: age, gender, or one or both of the underlying diagnoses? Perhaps some or all. He would have to go from univariate analysis to multivariable analyses to discern the real predictors of the difference.

If hospitalized men were more likely to be older than hospitalized women in this region, once the analysis corrected for gender, perhaps age would disappear as a predictor. The other differences would remain – the key difference.

Twenty minutes later Jake completed the final analysis, still completely absorbed in his computer. Deb and Mary were making plans to stop in a market in Sevilla, and the kids were playing games on their phones. Chris slept.

Jake could see that the odds ratio was now 3.9 for the diagnosis of either diabetes or heart failure. Patients with either diagnosis were almost four-fold more likely than controls to be admitted *after* the explosion. Age and gender were no longer significant, and both of the two diagnoses remained the only significant predictors for recent hospitalizations, still with a small probability of a chance observation, less than one percent.

"Chris, can I show you something?" Jake asked, touching Chris' shoulder to wake him.

Mary and Deb moved to allow the men to sit near each other.

"What do you make of that, Jake? Why would diabetes and heart failure patients be more prone to a hospital stay after an explosion when they were not directly injured?"

"I don't know. Perhaps we need more details about them. Maybe the drugs they're being treated with are the real issues, or the dose of insulin or special medications for coronary artery disease. At this point I can only speculate, but I'll pass this on to Elizabeth – after our day at the bullfights."

Chris gave a thumbs-up sign.

Jake finally put away his laptop, just in time for a full-course lunch, which was being served. The mood lifted as Jake joined in. He enjoyed letting the numbers go for the time being and tried to cheer up Deb by offering her his dessert.

Jake's cellphone ring caused a sudden derailment of the levity. "Jake, are you and Chris doing well? Safe?"

"Of course, Elizabeth. Why do you ask?" Deb rolled her eyes directly at Jake and turned to face out the window.

Elizabeth described a recent bombing at their hotel, the Hotel Isabella.

"It must have happened after we left. We're on the AVE headed for Sevilla and had planned to stay overnight after the late afternoon bullfight. What do you make of the incident?"

"Jake, I'm puzzled, but clearly there are too many coincidences. I'm not sure why. But you, Chris, and your families appear to be in harm's way. If you want, I can have your things transported to another hotel quietly and ask the local authorities to provide special protection. I recommend it."

"If you think we need to be that cautious, sure, go ahead." Jake was nervous at this point and felt the beginning of a headache. He reached for the ibuprofen capsules in the pocket of his jacket.

The three other adults stared at Jake, obviously sensing trouble from his strained look.

"I'll call you later with details about where you should go upon return to Barcelona. My preference is to have you in my hotel."

"Thanks, Elizabeth. By the way, I have some information for you. Not sure what it means, but the uninjured people who were hospitalized within two days after the rail station explosion were over-represented by those with underlying heart disease or diabetes. My analyses show a significant difference compared to baseline, pre-explosion rates."

"What additional information will help inform you further, Jake?"

"Details about the patients recently hospitalized with diabetes or heart disease versus similar patients hospitalized before the explosion would be good including the drugs they were receiving and details about any other underlying illnesses."

"I'll have that sent to you as soon as possible by email. As an aside, I received a call from Javier Gonzalez that power to a University Hospital's cardiac catheterization lab froze for 20 seconds and was restored spontaneously. It probably means nothing but made us nervous for a while.

"I hope you'll be able to enjoy the day given this update. I'm sorry, but I felt you should know about the Hotel Isabella bombing. I'll get back to you in a few hours. I'll arrange your arrival for late tonight or tomorrow, your choice. If tonight, I hope you can meet me to go over the data you have gathered. One more thing: be careful, my friend."

Jake pressed the call-off button, took a deep breath, and summarized the conversation.

"There's been a small explosion outside of our hotel. A few people suffered minor injuries, but no one was seriously hurt. The lobby and restaurant will need major work. Elizabeth has arranged to move our things to a new hotel with increased security. We can return either tonight to the new hotel or tomorrow as planned."

"It doesn't make a bit of sense to go to a bullfight in Sevilla if we need to return to Barcelona to a new hotel. How do we know we'll be safe in Sevilla? We also may need time to decide how and when we leave Spain," said Deb.

"I agree with Deb," said Mary, looking for affirmation from Chris. "I don't feel good about staying."

Jake nodded affirmatively, "The children won't like it. We'll have to explain it all to them."

In the half-hour it took to reach the station at Madrid, Jake and Chris reviewed the events with the teenagers, who didn't fuss about the change of plans. A new adventure awaited them in England. They had stories to tell from the Spanish trip already.

As the train pulled away, Jake noticed a man dressed in black clothes and wearing dark glasses, yelling at the conductor from the small platform between two cars. He looked as though he had missed his stop by the way he was gesturing to the station. Jake recognized the man from an uneasy encounter earlier as he exited the rest room. The man did not enter but instead fixed his gaze on Jake. Lord! I'm spooking myself over nothing, thought Jake, trying to regain equanimity.

The station master in Madrid did not argue about the exchange of return tickets and informed the group that the next train to Barcelona would arrive in forty minutes.

After being seated on the return train, Jake opened his laptop to check his email. *More Patient Data* sat waiting in his inbox, sent by Elizabeth.

Jake opened the new database and was pleased with the degree of clinical details provided on each patient. He set up a file of new patients – those admitted with diabetes or heart disease since the explosion on the railroad station – and a separate one of similar patients in the control time period, those with these two diagnoses hospitalized in the two-week period *before* the explosion. The newer database included only those patients at or near the rail station who had no traumatic injury yet required hospitalization or an emergency room visit.

In a separate email from Elizabeth, Jake received the name and address of the new hotel – Hotel Picasso, where she and her husband were staying. She went on to explain that security would be very high, they could meet to discuss updates, and that she had arranged for local contacts to move their belongings. They would stay on the fifth floor, one level above Elizabeth.

Now to see the patient differences and note if anything new fell out as significant, thought Jake, unsure of what he would find.

In about 20 minutes, Jake had his results. He was elated but puzzled.

"Chris, what do you make of this?" Jake passed the laptop across the aisle for Chris to see the data. "Among the non-injured patients who were hospitalized after the explosion, 85 percent were either diabetic with an insulin pump or were heart patients with either a pacemaker or defibrillator implanted."

"I suppose these are the more serious patients, Jake. These must be the more brittle diabetics with fluctuating blood-sugar levels and the heart patients with rhythm issues worse off than the usual diabetic and heart patients – perhaps more susceptible to stress."

"Probably so," said Jake, noting that now the odds ratio for each was five, and both were statistically significant.

"There is another more ominous consideration, Jake," said Chris. "What if cyber terrorists have created a malware program to interfere with medical equipment, in this case cardiac pacemaker devices and insulin pumps? Each device has tiny chips and programs to keep them functional. I've seen friendly cyber hackers at national conventions show how easily it could be done. I've been serving as lead on the hospital's cyber-security task force, and this is an entirely plausible possibility."

"So the immediate victims would be diabetics with a programmable pump for insulin and heart patients with a programmable device such as a pacemaker," concluded Jake. Patients with either diagnosis were five times more likely to be hospitalized in the period after the explosion than those controls from the period before the explosion. He could hardly contain himself.

"Among the visiting dignitaries to Barcelona, many could be innocent victims of medical device malware. Elizabeth needs to know our thinking.

"At the very least we have enough information to conclude that medical equipment may be at risk of cyber terror, that more may be coming, and that cyber counterintelligence needs to work immediately to assess the risk," said Jake. "I'm not even sure now that the brief disruption of a cardiac cath lab was accidental."

"A key question for Elizabeth," said Chris, "is, what's next?"

Jake pressed Elizabeth's number; he would ask to speak with cyber experts in Spain.

# XIX

In a remote booth at Café Gaude, a beaming Ramón proudly held out a large business envelope and presented it to Diana. "I have a pleasant surprise for you." Both were enjoying a cappuccino as part of the morning's meeting.

She grasped the envelope and opened it to see that seven enlarged photographs were enclosed. One by one she pulled them out, observing the faces in the pictures with both dread and excitement. Her nemesis, MI-5 agent Foster, was talking over breakfast with a middle-aged man in four of the photos; in the fifth and sixth photos, the couple was kissing, passionately, not as business associates. She banged her fist on the table.

"When and where were these taken, Ramón?"

"The first six were taken at the Hotel Isabella. The last photo of the agent and her husband was taken a little later in the day the Hotel Picasso. I have some friends on the wait staff at both places. I have learned that agent Foster has a disabled husband, and as you can clearly observe she appears to be burning the candle at both ends." Pointing to Elizabeth's rear end, he said, "Look where the professor's hand is resting.

"I followed up ninety minutes later with an incendiary token of our hospitality at the Hotel Isabella, as you suggested. I'm not sure yet what damage occurred or whether the physicians were affected, but the important point is that your wish has come true! The MI-5 agent *is* here, and we are tracking her every move. My guess is that the two physicians and their families will leave hurriedly tonight or tomorrow, leaving your MI-5 agent in town, alone but for her wheelchair-bound husband."

"Please make two sets of copies for me, Ramón. Imagine the response of agent Foster's husband reviewing the photographs. And the scandal at MI-5 will be delicious! Similarly, one never knows, but the wife of the Stanford physician may take exception to seeing her husband in an amorous embrace, his hand on that attractive ass."

"She may know nothing about this. Even if everything is platonic, a spouse who receives this enlarged photograph will have some doubt about the other's commitment to the marriage. Any woman knows this.

"Please continue surveillance on both parties, the MI-5 agent and both physicians. When we deliver copies of the photographs to their hotel rooms, agent Foster and the Stanford professor should be so distracted that both may focus on their respective departures. This will be of some comfort for me as I plan to neutralize agent Foster. And to think they don't even know we're here!"

"I'll plan to visit her tonight, and I would like your assistance, Ramón. I need your help in distracting her husband, moving him away from the room at their hotel. This woman is the person responsible for the death of my sister. I need revenge, an eye for an eye. I want nothing in my way. I hate her. The element of surprise is on our side, and I have a plan." Diana seemed at peace with this statement, thinking of her sister, mother, her grandmother, her father and uncle.

"Whatever you want, Diana. I'll help you in any way." Ramón was happy that Diana was pleased. He was a trusted player in the big league, and he envisioned a big payoff as a result.

"I know that I can count on you, Ramón. This is an unexpected aside, requiring some of our effort. Nevertheless, we can't lose sight of our mission here. Time is running out." It's difficult, and I don't want to be distracted, she thought. Sometimes fate brings surprise guests to the party, she mused.

"The test, the first experiment at the train station went well. The effects we wanted were accomplished. The authorities have no idea what is really going on, or who is behind it. Kleïs's program could affect the medical devices of those within one kilometer of the train station – ingenious. We are prepared for the new targets. We'll discuss the second experiment later.

"The explosion today at the Hotel Isabella will be quite confusing to the national meeting planners and will unexpectedly help us. However, our next big operation phase is only one day away and will lead to major international consequences. If all the dominos fall, we all win, and a new international order will have been born.

"A key issue for you, Ramón, is to be sure that the exchange of international funds flows smoothly. No interrupted payments for our supporters, no failure at any phase. This is critical to our long-term goals. I added a second step in the transfer to slow down any possible tracking, and that is why you are key to this success."

"No problem, Diana. I'm a small team player in this operation but delighted to help you and your colleagues. We're pleased to be a part of this team. It has been a pleasure for me and Pépe."

---

Later in the morning, Panos, posing as an international finance businessman at the Banco Iberica, was dressed neatly in a dark suit with a lime green tie and a starched white shirt. He graciously thanked the vice president of international transfers for his help, signed the agreement for a 0.05 percent transfer fee, and 1.8 million euros moved effortlessly from Corsica to Spain.

He awaited his Spanish colleague who would in turn make the second transfer to the Banco Iberica in Madrid. Panos imagined that this was a great day for Wil Cabezudo, for the entire transaction was costing minutes of his time, and the bank profited 900 euros!

In response to the V.P.'s question if he would wait for the second transfer, Panos said,

"No need to. My colleague will handle the next transfer, and please, Señor, help him in any way." They both rose, shook hands, and Wil Cabezudo escorted Panos to the front door of the bank, making a small bow as Panos exited the building.

---

Twenty-seven minutes later, on cue, Ramón arrived in the bank wearing a tan suit, light blue shirt, and dark blue tie and carrying an expensive briefcase. He wore tinted glasses as was his custom when he wished to avoid drawing attention to his eyes. Introducing himself by an alias, he met Cabezudo and signed the forms that had been prepared.

Ramón anticipated the question about where the transfer would be going and did his best to respond to the surprise of the vice president on hearing that Madrid was not the final destination. He told Cabezudo the final arrangements would require another 48 hours.

"Would it be acceptable to hold the money in a private account in Barcelona, accessible only to me?"

"Of course, sir. We're here to help any way we can, but I will have to charge you for each transfer, one for the transfer to Barcelona today and one whenever you move the money from this account. But because of your doing business in our bank, I can offer a discount on the second transfer. You may also log in with a secure password and make the final transfer yourself if you choose."

"Not a problem for me or my business associates, Senŏr Cabezudo. Now, where do I sign for today's transaction?"

When all the details of the transfer to a local account were managed, Cabezudo escorted his client to the front of the bank and graciously offered a final handshake.

On his way to Tio Pépe's, Ramón called his friend. "The transfer has been made according to plans."

"Que Bueno! Wonderful, Ramón," replied an excited Pépe. "We need to be cautious now. I'm more aware of the need to be absolutely sure of all details of our plan, especially after losing contact with the two physicians on the train. Timing is critical for us to achieve our special goal."

Ramón made a second call on his cell phone to Diana. "All is well, amiga, and Icarus is pleased." This was his code for the transactions, indicating that the cash was flying to its sunny destination. In an encouraging tone he continued, "You have nothing to worry about, and you can plan to carry out your personal vendetta. I'll contact you later this afternoon to confirm exact times."

# X X

J avier and Toni took furious notes in an intense meeting with two
Spanish government cyber-terror analysts. Wearing black t-shirts,
jeans, and running shoes, both young men appeared free of any care and
barely in their twenties. They were widely known in cyber circles as
Batman and Robin. Computer nerds, thought Toni. Both were thin, and
he imagined them to be vegetarians who never saw a gym or barbell.
Neither had parts in their long hair. The only difference in the closely
cloned cyber wonks was that one was several inches taller than the other.
Nevertheless, they had developed important portfolios with an impressive
series of accomplishments in counter-terror and discovery responses.

From background research, Toni had learned that Nach Romanos was
twenty-two years old, the taller of the two, and an expert in computer
games since early childhood. He was the author of several financially
successful war games, beginning with an animated game of the Spanish
Civil War, which Toni now owned. The game came complete with
military and paramilitary leaders for the Republic, the nationalists who
plotted the coup, and communist activists. Toni gathered that when Nach

acquired wealth, he sought new challenges rather than material possessions. His latest interest was cyber terror. He told them he sought work with the government after he had applied to some large industries without success. His talents had been quickly recognized and embraced.

Diego Figueroa wore a silver nose ring and was a known hack genius. Toni's investigation into Figueroa established that the 24-year-old had earned a prosperous income by selling his findings to individual companies for a living. Those companies readily bought the information so they could repair existing targets before a competitor or another non-state cyber terror unit discovered the vulnerabilities. One report noted that Figueroa had once been arrested and offered a choice – use his talents in jail or on Spanish government counter-cyber-terror activities.

Nach and Diego became very close friends as well as respected colleagues. Toni's reports referred to them by their given names, but in his mind, Toni referred to them a Batman and Robin, maybe sarcastically but mostly because few agents could even remember their first names.

In the meeting with Javier and Toni, Batman and Robin said that the information forwarded by Jake Evans was critical in pointing to cyber terror. The epidemiological link of hospitalized patients without trauma to malfunctioning medical devices was insightful. Otherwise, the authorities would have been misled for some time into thinking the bombing at the train station was just another ETA provocation. Most of the medical authorities assumed that those without trauma had suffered from stress, the anxiety and fear of being part of a bombing terror act. People with weak hearts might have abnormal rhythms in the face of a bombing just as diabetics may show fluctuations in blood sugar from the action of stress hormones in a terrorist situation. But it was not stress – it was cyber hacking of their medical devices. "Now we need to know what follows. What is their true focus of interest, and how severe is the threat to the public?" said Batman.

Toni was surprised, "Isn't this bad enough? We know that two state dignitaries have medical devices. Aren't they the real targets?"

"Possibly, but the attack is novel and sophisticated," responded Batman. "And it was followed by an apparent loss of power in a cardiac catheterization lab in a university hospital – even if temporary.

"Let's suppose they want to damage a vulnerable infrastructure. For sake of argument I'll call it the public health infrastructure. So they pick on the medical arena, first programmable devices, then larger radiology equipment and hospital energy sources. Pretty soon the public loses confidence in medical, nursing, and public health authorities, and the entire network of systems of public health. What would be a next step if your goal is to take down the public health infrastructure?" He paused briefly and asked, "What could the effect be?"

Robin raised his hand. "In the U.S., a 2003 summer blackout affected millions of citizens for two days and cost $6 billion," he said. He went on to say that 50 million people lost power. Food in refrigerators spoiled, gas pumps failed, and public transportation faltered. "What is at risk is an erosion of confidence in government, significant financial losses and social disorder."

Robin went on to describe an attack on the electrical grid on Saudia Aramco when the shamoon worm instantly destroyed the hard drives of 30,000 computers in the state-run oil company. Major water, oil, and electrical grids were shown to be vulnerable. "Terror creates fear, and people want a return to order, even if order comes at a price of major change."

Cracking his knuckles, Javier nodded, recalling discussions of cyber terror at recent training sessions. "We have been warned that both grid observation and control systems are increasingly vulnerable, increasingly connected to the internet."

Toni nodded. This makes sense, he thought. A hacker could throw a vulnerable system out of phase by cyber-attacks on the control system, interrupting the electricity and blocking the flow of vital information. And that's just one example he had come up with in an instant. The chaos that could be plotted and planned with time was unfathomable.

Batman said that too many countries had not responded to the earlier attacks with updated safeguards, in part because they were costly. He reminded the group that the Stuxnet computer worm, thought to be designed by U.S. and Israel and used to damage the Iranian nuclear program, had escaped accidentally from the Natanz nuclear plant, probably on someone's personal computer, and had entered the public domain. "In 2012, Flame, a malware that attacks computers running Microsoft Windows was discovered, yet few private companies and few countries have new safeguards against these known malware products. When it comes to cyber terror too few nations and too few large companies have adequate risk management programs."

Batman appeared frustrated with that last statement, thought Toni, possibly reflecting his unanswered warnings and unmet budgetary needs.

"That is why we ask what's next, why we play the what-if scenarios," said Robin. "We don't just ask what is the worst incident we have seen with malware. We ask, what is the worst incident we can imagine, one even more serious than any previously described." He seemed to be pleading for understanding.

Toni agreed. He recalled a conversation earlier that day with a banker in Barcelona. The bank vice president said that one client had asked if anyone was hacking his account. He was asking out of an abundance of caution. However, the banker's own cyber-security team could see that a second party had been viewing the man's transactions with malware modified from Gauss. An account worth 1.8 million euros was being viewed. The V.P., Señor Cabazudo, reminded Toni that Gauss had been discovered in 2012 by the Russian Kaspersky Lab and designed to gather information on banking transactions, often stealing login information from emails and social networking websites.

Toni asked if Batman thought that the banking hacker and medical device hacking might be related. After all, 1.8 million euros was a lot of money, useful for criminals on terror missions.

"We have to consider it seriously," Batman answered. "Based on what we have so far, I still favor a basic grid as the ultimate target, to disrupt medical care in a major way."

Toni suggested thinking about what health-related grid would be especially vulnerable and terrifying if hacked: water control, nuclear power, oil or electrical grids. "But should we now add banking?" he inquired.

"For the most part, hacking into banks is for the purpose of stealing money, to secure funds for nefarious operations," Batman replied. He proposed that if the two events in Barcelona were related, perhaps the flow of money to support the interruption of vital health infrastructure was the connection.

"Let's suppose that an electrical grid and/or public health infrastructure is the target. What would interruption mean for the medical profession?"

Robin emphasized that the goal of any terror event was to frighten the public, disrupt government leadership and management, and create doubt about the leadership. "For some reason, these people want to overthrow the existing government and substitute it with another. And we don't know who the cyber terrorists are or what new replacement government they have in mind or why."

Clasping his fingers behind his head and leaning back in his chair, Batman mused, "Imagine no first responders, no police, no firemen, no ambulances, no exchange of medical information including results of x-rays, heart monitoring in ICUs, oxygen delivery systems. Then, no radiotherapy to treat cancer, no pharmacy checks on drugs or drug interactions. No ability to stop dangerous heart rhythms with defibrillators. It could get serious fast."

He continued, "What if, in addition, any testing is available is erroneous? The blood count is reported to be low and an unnecessary transfusion is ordered. The blood match is reported to be fine but is in error. Then a patient who needs no blood is given a transfusion that causes a deadly reaction."

Batman continued, "Imagine the wrong dose of a drug, the wrong drug, an erroneous and lethal radiation dose for a tumor, a spuriously high reading on oxygenation and failure to recognize that more is needed. Anyway, you guys get the idea, it may be all about infrastructure."

Toni felt a sickening Eureka moment, "They're after the entire health information system!"

Winking at his partner, Robin exclaimed, "Holy Aesculapius! What do we do now?" Both men grinned.

Javier and Toni thanked the men for their time and attention. As he opened the door to leave, under his breath, Toni whispered, "We should all head to the Bat Cave."

# XXI

T he next step for Ramón was to assist Diana to mete out justice against MI-5 agent Elizabeth Foster. He had promised. His contacts had identified her hotel and room number. Initially he hadn't planned on her husband being with her, but when he learned that the barrister was disabled in a wheelchair, he concluded the situation shouldn't pose a major obstacle.

Ramón had convinced the maître d' that he was a close friend of the couple and wanted to surprise them with two bottles of champagne and a box of flowers for their anniversary. Could he know the name of the restaurant where they would have plans this evening? For his help, would a 30-euro tip be sufficient?

The maître d' gladly received the money and mentioned they would be dining in their suite tonight. It would be his pleasure to take the order for the champagne and flowers and present them at dinner.

"Absolutely," said a thankful Ramón. "At what hour will the meals be delivered?"

"The English couple plans to eat early – precisely 7:00 p.m."

"You've been extremely helpful, my friend," said Ramón, "Very cordial. I'll be sure to arrange for my gifts to be delivered in time for dinner, barring any last minute surprises."

He then began to formulate detailed plans for the evening's events. It could get complicated. Timing was everything.

Later on, just before seven, Ramon entered the hotel. In a gray suit with a white shirt and a green-and-gray striped tie, Ramón was wearing tinted glasses and approached the young waiter in front of the elevator in the lobby. With a warm smile he asked if by chance the man was taking the meals to Elizabeth Foster, a close friend. Somewhat surprised, the man asked, "How did you know"?

Ramón said that he had arranged the special delivery of two bottles of champagne and a box of flowers.

"Oh, yes, these are right here on the cart!"

"If it is no trouble, may I join you? I had not planned on being available tonight." He held his hand out to present a five-euro bill.

That's not necessary, Señor."

"I insist," said Ramón. "I was a waiter for years before I went into business. Please accept this."

The man was grateful and apologetically said he had a bottle of wine that he needed to deliver to another guest on the second floor. But he welcomed Ramón to join him.

"It will only take a moment."

"Wonderful," exclaimed Ramón as both entered the elevator.

When the doors opened on the second level, Ramón motioned to the waiter to go ahead. As he did, Ramón unleashed a brutal blow to the man's cheek, knocking him unconscious immediately. He fell to the floor, and Ramón pulled him into a cloak room, removed his outfit and put it on himself, then bound the waiter's hands behind his waist.

Proceeding to the fourth floor, Ramón moved down the hall and around a corner from room 421 at the Hotel Picasso. The gentle knock he delivered was followed by several seconds of silence. After several more seconds, the door opened and a quiet conversation followed.

"Barrister Foster, your meal is here."

"You're a different waiter than last night. I thought he was still on duty."

"He was to be, sir, but he had a family problem come up," said the disguised Ramón.

"So sorry to hear that. My wife will be disappointed. We bonded with the young gentleman over stories of his travel in London."

"I understand completely. That man has a bright future ahead of him, with so much talent and charm. The rest of us hope someday to be almost as good as he is," Ramón chuckled and went on. "I hope you'll both enjoy the wonderful seafood dinner. Our sea bass is as good as it gets. Oh my, I left some special gifts from the hotel management on a table by the elevator when I took a call from the chef. Let me present those to you."

Ian replied a hesitant "Yes" to the request, and was wheeled into the hallway. The waiter placed a box of long-stemmed flowers on Ian's lap and handed him two bottles of champagne, one for each hand.

With lightning speed, Ramón ran around the wheelchair, grasped its handles from behind, and pulled a confused Ian Foster farther into the hallway and towards the open elevator door. But there was no elevator there. Ian reached up to punch him but managed only to dislodge Ramón's glasses, looking directly into his eyes.

Ramón whipped the chair in a circular move with Ian now facing the elevator opening. The open shaft, which he had arranged right before taking his place in the hallway, greeted the disoriented occupant of the wheelchair, who was still grasping the gifts. Ramón pushed Foster into the void with all his might. As the wheelchair crashed into the wall on one side of the elevator, both bottles dropped first, then Ian hit the elevator shaft with a loud thud.

Looking away from the elevator to replace his fallen spectacles, Ramón whispered, "I have already hit the down button for you. Have a nice evening."

# XXII

E lizabeth Foster called to her husband from the bedroom of the suite, "Ian, who's at the door?" Hearing no answer, she raced towards the front door, instinctively pulling her pistol out.

Poking her head out of the open doorway, she saw a woman get off the far elevator with a gun in her hand. Diana Kontos looked shocked to see Elizabeth only five meters away from her.

Elizabeth could not see Ian but moved back behind a couch in their suite just as two bullets soared by above her head. At the moment two men entered the floor from the stairwell. To Elizabeth's utter surprise Diana immediately retreated down the stairs, passing by the men.

Elizabeth slowly peeked around the couch, saw the two men on the floor in the hallway and cautiously stood up, her left hand clasping her right wrist to steady the gun. She rose with her arms outstretched. She spoke in English and asked them to identify themselves as she patted each down quickly. Neither had a weapon, but both carried canisters of mace. She identified herself and asked why they were on the floor.

The men told her that they had received an anonymous call that a crazed, possibly armed woman, was on this floor, banging on the door of one of the rooms. The male caller also said that a man had attacked one of the waiters on the second floor. "We saw that the waiter had been mugged and tied up in an unused cloak room. His outfit was taken from him, and he sustained several bruises to his face in the scuffle."

As Elizabeth approached the stairwell, she saw the empty wheelchair on its side next to an open elevator shaft.

"Oh, my God! No! Ian!! Ian!!"

"Help! Help me!" A raspy voice called from the elevator shaft.

Elizabeth peered into the dark space and screamed for the two security men to help.

She knew the voice. The shaft was dark, but she could make out the outline of her husband holding the thick elevator cable.

Elizabeth dialed the front desk, desperate for medical assistance and more security. Anything to help.

Both security men lay flat on the ground, reaching for Ian. They told him to continue to hold onto the cable. Each grasped his belt hoping to pull him up.

Ian Foster was exhausted, moaning in pain and breathing loudly, but Elizabeth sensed his determination to hang on, to live.

As the security men hoisted him up a few feet, Ian was able to move one hand up the cable, then the other, slowly lifting his body.

With renewed effort, Ian's chest made it above the floor and into the hallway. The security duo continued to pull his belt and hoisted his dead legs fully into the hallway. Ian was panting like a marathon runner crossing the final line.

"Ian! Thank God you're okay. Who did this?"

"Elizabeth," he gasped, "It was a man. He was Spanish, muscular." He paused to breathe. "He had tinted glasses, but I think his eyes were totally purple! I thought I was dead." He took in a huge loud breath. "But I held onto the cables for dear life!"

"We'll need more security tonight; I'll ask the local authorities for help. In the meantime, you need medical attention. If you are cleared of any medical issue, you'll go directly to the airport. I'll arrange a secure flight home."

The hotel security men helped Ian back to his upright wheelchair.

Two more security men arrived along with a physician summoned by the hotel. Ian was briefly examined in his room by the hotel doctor before being transported to the hospital. The true waiter was found on another floor, they learned, with a bruised cheek, obviously the victim of the imposter.

Accompanying Ian to the hospital, Elizabeth called Jake to report what had happened. "Jake, he had completely purple eyes, no white areas."

"Purple eyes?" Jake repeated loudly. "His cornea must have been deliberately colored." Elizabeth could hear talking in the background from Jake's hotel room. She thought it was his son.

"Dad, I know where that man works," she heard.

# XXIII

In a square office above a café on Calle Gaude, Kleïs was intensely observing two open computer screens. Eureka! She had cracked the entrance to a key database, the last of three previously secured programs she had worked on for almost a year. She had found a way! "Spain today, France tomorrow, and Israel soon."

The local initiative would be disturbing and confusing enough, she imagined. But the elegance of the new plan would be unique. A few had tried, but none had succeeded before. She would deplete their resources, suck the energy from them, confuse their defenses, and terrify the public who would demand a change of leadership. Patient information would be switched. The embarrassment to physicians would be great. A swelling loss of patient confidence would follow. Labs would report erroneous findings. Operating rooms would be assigned to patients scheduled for another. First responders would be given erroneous addresses!

At the next meeting in Corsica, Kleïs would profusely thank the collaborative attendees from Russia, North Korea, and Latvia who opened her horizons to new hacking skills, but of course she would demur on giving them her own embellishments to the computer hacking programs. It might be difficult initially, but in the end, they would understand. They would recognize her sophisticated enhancements to the Trojan she created, which could also seize control of an infected computer's mouse and capture screenshots.

In fact, by then, they would have read about the entire attack. She and Diana would be welcomed by delegates to the future International Days of Corte. And they wouldn't be simply talking or wishing to topple some governments, they would have shown actual results. Then they would be off to an extended vacation in Alexandria and perhaps later to the Greek Islands, maybe even the Aegean home of Sappho.

She felt good and decided to extend her joy by looking at the transfer of funds at the local bank. Of course she would need to hack into the account, but that was no new obstacle.

What she observed was puzzling, alarming, and unexpected. She slapped the table. Damn it!

The sound of the lock turning brought her back. Diana Kontos burst into the room, furious. "Kleïs, I don't know what went wrong, just when I almost had the MI-5 agent."

"What happened? What do you mean?"

"Ramón was supposed to take her husband to the roof and push him over the edge, but I never saw Ramón. I only saw a wheelchair overturned by an empty elevator shaft. Our timing should have been perfect, I had Sasha's killer in my sights. She had her weapon drawn, and I don't know why." She described how she fired two shots at Elizabeth, who crouched behind a sofa and that, to her surprise, security agents were there exactly when she arrived, as if waiting for her.

"Now they know I'm in Barcelona, and the freedom we had is over. It may jeopardize our hopes to complete the task."

"How is Ramón?" asked Kleïs.

"I tried to reach him on my way here, but he never picked up. If he wasn't caught by authorities, surely he'll call."

"Come over here, Diana. I am not at all convinced that Ramón and Pépe were victims of police activity. I've been following up on the money transfer and saw something curious, then very, very disturbing. I hacked into the transactions of the Banco Iberica and I noticed that the movement of euros to Corsica and to Spain went smoothly. But the second transfer was stalled here in Barcelona. It did not go on to pay for the volunteers as planned. I can't find the transfer to the Madrid bank, only a secure site here in Barcelona with no immediate access to a name or amount."

Both women uttered the same word in unison, "Ramón!"

"Kleïs, can you see whose account the money sits in now?"

A few keystrokes later, Kleïs confirmed that it was deposited into the account of an alias that Ramón had used in the past.

"I've seen deception before, Kleïs, and I've had to deal with hypocrisy and greed. Ramón will find that his future is limited. That bastard will wish he never met me!"

Diana reminded Kleïs of the time when an alleged friend, Ata Atuk, showed his true stripes, arranging an assassin to kill Sasha and her. He had planned to sell the twins' bioengineered *Staphylococcus* strain to terrorists for a huge sum of money. But Ata was the one surprised in the end. In a vendetta to repay the loss of trust, Ata was paralyzed with a poison dart containing botulism toxin, and, two years later, he remained on a respirator in Germany, paralyzed, unable to breathe on his own, and unable to see. His eyes had also been injected with a highly antibiotic resistant strain of *Staphylococcus aureus*.

"Ramón must have planned for my death or capture by notifying the security personnel at the hotel, Kleïs."

"And he intended to keep the money. He has to pay for this," said Kleïs, who imagined a tragic fate in exchange for his deceit and disloyalty. "We know his Achilles heel," she blurted out in anger. She looked back at Diana. "Your expertise will now be unleashed on this traitor!" She slapped her knee in frustration. "He won't see this coming. His entire body will be in uncontrollable overdrive on a path to crashing. Something worse than pain on his way to nothingness."

# XXIV

S till limping after his run-in with Ramón, Eduardo nervously
hobbled into Tio Pépe's. With obvious deference to Ramón, he
apologized for being a day late but said he was pleased to pay his debt.

Ramón smiled and approached Eduardo with a gentle tap on the
cheek. "Buenos días, mi amigo. I am pleased to see you," he said. He
pointed to the back room where they had met only two days earlier.

Eduardo felt vulnerable, barely hearing the "Buenos días." He had
suffered substantial loss of hearing on one side, the result of Ramón's
cruel puncture of his ear drum. Eduardo walked toward the room, the
scene of Ramón's sadistic action.

Since entering the drug trade as a middleman, he was a master of
subservience to all, a trusted member of the team. He knew that life was
not always valued in this business, and on some runs kept a small gun
strapped at his ankle. The gun had originally belonged to his father, a
marksman with a cunning personality, always advising his son to prepare
for the worst but to remain calm at all times, never giving an adversary
the sense that he was aggressive or even vengeful. Eduardo saw the

weapon as an extreme form of insurance should he get cornered, when there might be no escape. In general, he avoided carrying a gun even when he and Ramón met. Talk was always preferred.

"I don't want any more trouble, Ramón, and I apologize for being late with the payment. You have been very tolerant of me, and it'll never happen again."

Ramón closed the heavy metal door behind them both, essentially creating a soundproof room.

When Ramón picked up a lead pipe with his left hand, Eduardo's nerves frazzled, as though he was having a flashback. "Please, no more pain. I'll never bother you again."

"People like you, Eduardo, never learn, always taking advantage of the situation, always pushing the relationships, and eventually breaking the trust. Like Judas, you let us down and eventually become a traitor. The world looks at the group of Eduardos and says it would be a better place without your type. Que lástima! What a shame!"

"No, please don't say that, Ramón. We can work together for the benefit of both of us. I've learned my lesson, forgive me."

Ramón seemed to change his mood and shrugged his shoulders. His face softened. "Well, okay. Let's have a drink, Eduardo, and maybe we can work things out. Please sit down, and I'll pour us each a shot of good whiskey to celebrate our new peace. How are your beautiful ladies?" Looking directly into Eduardo's eyes with a wide smile, he slid his right hand down over his thigh and grasped his own crotch.

He placed the lead pipe on the floor and walked to a cabinet where he took out a bottle of whiskey and a couple of shot glasses. Sitting down, he poured one drink for Eduardo and one for himself. "Salúd, mi amigo."

As both men toasted the new relationship, Eduardo relaxed slightly but felt unsure as to what was coming next.

Ramón lifted his head to drain the contents of the shot glass while opening the drawer of the table in front of his seat and pulling out a revolver.

"I'll give you one more chance, Eduardo. You can prove to me and everyone in our organization that you are a reliable business man. If you agree to give me 5,000 more euros for the trouble you have caused me and my colleagues, tonight, I'll call us even. What do you say?"

Without a second's hesitation, Eduardo answered. "Very kind, Ramón. Very kind indeed. I'll honor your wish and return with the money tonight. Thank you so much." He stretched out his arm to reach Ramón's hand, as though a deal had been reached. But Ramón's glanced away. Eduardo's gesture went unanswered.

Ramón released his grip on the weapon and it dropped in the drawer in front of him. "Would you mind arriving at about eight o'clock tonight, Eduardo? I have a busy day planned for tomorrow and would like to get this out of the way."

"No problema. Esta noche, a las ochos. I'll be on time for you, Ramón, and am deeply appreciative of your understanding." He reached out with his right hand to shake hands with a willing Ramón.

"Let's have another drink to seal our friendship, Eduardo."

Eduardo knew that Ramón had a concealed weapon in the drawer and did his best to smile appreciatively at his enemy. He wasn't at all sure how he would get the money he needed for Ramón but knew that his only chance to survive was to agree with anything requested. With the new demand he knew that there was no end in sight, that Ramón would continue to bleed him financially, continue to threaten him and his family. He might even attempt to kidnap his wife and daughter or worse, rape them. For today, however, he needed to get some money and avoid the immediate threat.

Eduardo returned home to the joyous greeting of his wife and daughter, both terrified about his earlier run-in with Ramón, the ongoing uncertainty, and the potential risks that would lie ahead. They'd been painfully aware of Ramón's frightful reputation - even before Eduardo was injured.

Eduardo told his daughter not to worry and said he and her mother would sit down over coffee and discuss how to manage the current problem. "Everything is OK, now, sweetheart. We are all safe." He kissed Núria's forehead, and she seemed satisfied.

With Núria out of hearing range, Eduardo reviewed possible options, highlighting the nagging concern that Ramón would never let go, would continue to threaten him and his family. As he sipped his coffee, his wife bent over him and wrapped both arms around his neck from the back of the chair.

They discussed running away to hide with various family members in other parts of Spain, developing new identities, allowing Eduardo to enter a new trade while escaping the drug arena. Facing Lourdes, Eduardo said, "We cannot stay here. They are predators on the savannah, lions continually stalking the wildebeest. We need to disappear."

Eduardo said that perhaps the best pathway ahead was to open new chapter, the three of them to moving to Majorca, initially with Eduardo's brother; but perhaps if they decided to stay on, he would find work there in his brother's restaurant outside of Palma.

Eduardo revisited his options and told his wife that he might try one more time to yield to Ramón's demand for more money. He expressed confidence to his wife about getting a loan to pay off his additional debt.

He had to get some business done to facilitate paying money to Ramón, but then also suggested that there was no reason to delay a wonderful new adventure. Even if he paid off the new request, a family visit to Majorca was a good idea. He must have appeared to his wife to have the sniffles. She suggested a trip to the Farmacia to treat his cold early before making his business arrangements. She was delighted that he quickly agreed.

"What happens, Eduardo, if you cannot get the money in time for Ramón?"

"My chances are good that everything will work out, dear," responded Eduardo. This was not a good time to review plan B, he thought. "Let me get something to clear my head out, and we'll be OK." In the face of the challenges ahead, resolute in the decision he saw as a pathway to freedom, he knew she was so proud of him.

Eduardo sought to appear comfortable to his wife with the threats from Ramón. He endeavored to be upbeat.

# XXV

F lanked by two armed security officers at the hospital, Ian Foster lay on the gurney, still shocked by his near-death experience. How close a call had he had! Why had he come to Barcelona, placing Elizabeth in harm's way? Both palms were gashed and bloody from grasping and sliding down the cables of the elevator, but his tendons were intact. He could move his fingers on both hands.

Elizabeth stood close. The neurologist continued his examination. Much of the skin of Ian's legs was bruised. The doctor tested for any new muscle weakness or loss of sensation. He tapped with a small rubber hammer to test the reflexes usually present in an intact spinal cord, and the cranial nerves that control eye movement, smelling, hearing and balance, facial sensation, the movement of the pharynx and tongue, and the ability to shrug the shoulders. All appeared to be working normally.

Breathing more rapidly and speaking more softly than normal, Ian remained alert. He knew his name, location, the date and time. The neurologist ordered an MRI of the head to rule out a brain contusion or collection of blood. He suggested keeping the barrister overnight for observation in a private room. The security team could be placed in an anteroom, the only access to the patient.

Ian had no plans to stay overnight. "I'm collateral damage but don't want to add more complications to my wife's mission," he said. If cleared, he would return immediately to the airport for a flight home. That way his wife could work without distraction. That decision was not up for discussion, case closed.

Ian entered the MRI machine headfirst. His large upper body moved slowly into the tubular space, and he heard the totally foreign sounds of the MRI in action: loud panting noises and strange pings, then high-pitched notes of irritating discord. There was a hollowness to this new world he entered, an anti-musical space. He closed his eyes to escape this uncomfortable place and tried to imagine a quiet beach on the coast of Italy, listening to the sonorous sound of waves breaking monotonously on the sand, sensing warm sun above and soft sand on his back. He would transport himself to that safe locale for twenty minutes, abandoning the aural and kinesthetic misery of modern medical technology. After all, the MRI was for reassurance. He had not hit his head. Doctors need reassurance, perhaps even more in his case. After all, he was a barrister, and his wife was an anti-terrorist agent.

Ten minutes into the test, the clamorous noise ceased abruptly, the lights went out, and a radiology technician rushed into the MRI room. Ian was surprised but remained still, careful to follow instructions. She asked if he was okay, apologized for the interruption, and said she didn't know what was happening. "No entiendo. No comprendo, Señor."

The technician pressed the lever to move the MRI table out of the magnet, but nothing happened. The magnet sat silent and unresponsive. Ian focused on his breathing, wondering if the tube surrounding his chest was restricting his inhalations in some way. Was he imagining shortness of breath? Would he wake up in a sweat from a terrifying nightmare? He needed to clear his head, to face reality. Worse things have happened, he thought; he needed to avoid panic. He would return to his placid, sandy beach on the Amalfi coast.

The technician called her supervisor and then security to help her pull the patient out of the enclosed area and onto the gurney. Elizabeth greeted him with a concerned look and placed her hand on his. She told him she was going to step out to phone the administrator. She was gone briefly and then returned.

"I'm told the hospital's generator was triggered by a blackout, that all lighting was out briefly, respirators failed, and ICU personnel were in a panic. Technicians are in the house and will address the issues now. They hope to resolve it all shortly. Such a widespread loss of power is unprecedented. The administrator says they'll call other hospitals for help if the problem persists."

"Help me get dressed and get to the airport, Elizabeth. This is a very serious development. You are facing the biggest crisis of your career. I need to be out of your way."

# XXVI

Worse news about the expansion of the cyber terror came with Elizabeth's phone call to Commander Gonzalez. The power to all area hospitals had been affected by the electrical outage. In each institution, the radiology imaging equipment was interrupted, and in a few hospitals without sufficiently large generators, the nurses had to manually bag the intubated patients on life-supporting respirators to maintain their oxygen levels. At least in one hospital the insulin pumps were failing, creating both elevated and dangerously low blood sugar levels; pacemaker devices were sputtering off and on, causing cardiac patients frightening intermittent heart rhythm problems.

Elizabeth's emotions ricocheted between terror and relief. She had nearly lost her husband, but thankfully, he seemed alert and safe now. She knew this assignment was a big deal, and she wanted desperately to seize Diana Kontos, a formidable opponent. She was at once full of fatigue, nervous energy, and focus. In Spain, she also felt very much alone.

"Javier, this latest volley hit home with my husband unable to complete the image of his brain. The MRI was hacked!" She went on to say that all medical equipment – large and small – would have to be reprogrammed or replaced.

All this rang true for Javier, having listened to the conjectures of Bat Man and Robin earlier. He sensed the extreme urgency for a quick and effective response from law enforcement. He also had a sense of history. "This case will make or break my career and Toni's," he said.

"Elizabeth, we face this just as the dignitaries are to arrive. One has a heart device, another an insulin delivery device to control diabetes. Perhaps others have devices I don't know about." He told her he had sent texts asking each to have the devices reprogrammed. "The aide to the prime minister, Joaquin Lopez, has contacted all dignitaries and told each that they could decline coming to the meeting, and we would understand and respect their decision. None want to miss it."

Elizabeth fought to hold back tears. "We have to catch these people, Javier!" She went on to say she suspected they might have other goals besides interrupting life at hospitals and harming dignitaries. "I bet your government soon will receive demands and related threats if certain milestones are not met."

"I'm sure you're right, Elizabeth. In the meantime Toni will be meeting me in a few minutes, and we'll update the aides to the president. Our forensic cyber team will try to reverse or neutralize the malware function. You're welcome to join us. I need to arrange a SWAT team to visit Tio Pépe's immediately."

"Thanks, Javier. I would like to join you as soon as possible. I want to arrange safe travel for my husband, then inform my two physician friends what is happening and ask for their perspectives. I assume they're planning to leave Barcelona as soon as possible."

Regret overwhelmed Elizabeth, a sense of loss as Jake prepared to depart Spain. She called his number.

"Jake!" was all she managed in a shaky voice.

"Elizabeth, what's wrong?"

She told him of the attempt on her husband's life and her surprise, life-threatening visit from Diana who escaped, again. She described the scene at the hospital, her husband's need to leave Spain, and her own need to join the law enforcement team for tonight's meeting. "Please meet me after the meeting, when I return to the hotel. I need to talk. I need you."

# XXVII

A mist in the air announced the start of a slight drizzle, and a thin haze formed halos around the street lamps. Toni glanced at his watch: 1:00 a.m. The sidewalks dampened as Javier, Elizabeth, and Toni arrived in front of Tio Pépe's, followed by two additional cars from Grupos Operatives Especiales de Seguridad, GOES, the SWAT team members. Toni had ordered that all wear bullet-proof vests. The SWAT team would be dressed in their typical armed forces tactical uniforms. Each member of the team would carry submachine guns or assault rifles. A few would carry flash or tear gas grenades. Across the street in an alley, a prostitute negotiated with her John, nodding, grasping his hand. Toni opened his car door. Rock music poured from two nearby bars, their doors open. Flashing white lights from one matched the bass guitar sounds emanating from inside.

A sign over the front door at Tio Pépe's simply said *Cerrada* – closed. The building sat dark and quiet. Two members of the SWAT team raced to the rear to secure all exits. A six-inch lock securing a latch to a large metal eye ensured that no one would be coming out the back way.

Nevertheless, the agents would stay in place until the mission was complete. That door would not be opened now. Toni and the other agents approached the front entrance.

Through the bare windows, the agents swept the main room with flashlights. Two bodies lay motionless near the bar, overturned stools next to them as though each had been in conversation when their lives were interrupted by violence. One man lay face up with his glass nearby. The other man lay face down. A rat scurried away, deterred by the intruding light.

"Open up!" yelled Toni "Abra!" But there was no response. With a battering ram Javier slammed the front door and the handle, snapping the lock. Toni gave the signal that it was time to enter. He pointed to the two agents on the left to secure that side of the room and the other two to take care of the right. He walked straight ahead with his weapon drawn. All was still, except for the stealth movements of the team.

All of the agents and Elizabeth had weapons aimed at the two men on the floor. Neither was breathing when the light came on, thick pools of purplish red blood could be seen oozing from obvious bullet wounds to each man's chest and abdomen. The acrid smell of stale blood filled the air. They bled out in seconds, thought Toni.

The murderers who did this wanted no witnesses left behind. One man's wallet was splayed open next to his hand with several bills inside. Money was not the motive.

Two SWAT members searched the front entrance and main room, while Toni approached the door to the small back room. He threw the door open and circled his flashlight around the stillness.

Toni hit the switch.

Sitting in a chair was a man with athletic, tattooed arms, his hands bound behind his back with plastic ties, and a black hood covering his head. A link chain was strung around his neck and was crudely fastened to the wall with an eye-hook. Bullet entrance wounds at the both knee caps still oozed blood. Toni lifted the hood using latex gloves. The man looked to be under 45 years and been tortured at the end of his life.

Suffocation was the likely cause of death. Duct tape wrapped around the mouth and nose would have made it impossible to breathe. Severe bruises at his wrists indicated he had tried frantically to free himself from the ties.

Javier followed Toni into the small room and took in the horrifying scene. "So much visible torture. This must be meant as a signal to any friend or associate of the dead man: Cross me, you'll be next, and it won't be pretty."

Toni nodded.

Just then something fell onto the floor and rolled a few centimeters.

"Oh, my God!" gasped Elizabeth. The man's left eye had been crudely removed with a sharp tool and had fallen from the top of his face. It was evident to Elizabeth that the dark color covering the white part of the man's eyes was not due to blood but to tattoos, as Ian had described his would-be assassin. He was the same man that Brice had seen on their night out.

Toni called for an ambulance and a forensic team with photography equipment to document the crime scene and to take fingerprints. Once the victims were identified, especially the man in the chair, Toni would schedule interviews with all known relatives and business contacts. They would also confiscate a laptop computer, some papers and a handgun in a drawer.

The team discussed the particulars of the scene. Javier suggested the man was likely a part of the establishment. But how had this man, probably no stranger to violence, been caught off guard? To Toni, the scene suggested that the dead man in the chair and his killer were acquainted. The bullet wounds were directly straight on. He must have been shot after he sat down in the chair.

"Perhaps a gang killing," said Toni, "a vivid message to the victim's colleagues, a vicious threat. Maybe it was a drug deal gone sour and this the warning."

"No need for you to stay, Elizabeth," said Javier. He pointed to one of the team members. "We'll escort you back to your hotel and call you tomorrow. Toni and I will remain here for the forensics team. You'll have security at the hotel, and you can let each know who can and cannot approach your room."

One of the SWAT team members at the entrance to the small office noted the blinking light indicating a phone voice message. Toni walked over with a new set of latex gloves and pressed the button to listen.

"You made a fatal mistake, Ramón," began the message. The female voice spoke in English, with a slight Middle Eastern accent, overtones of British, not American influence. "You are not safe, my old friend, and there is no place on earth for you to hide from me, you stupid bastard! Your greed and your disloyalty are your undoing. You will be running the rest of your brief life. Your recent financial windfall will never buy you security. You can bank on it!"

# XXVIII

Two security agents were stationed by the elevator on the fourth floor in the Hotel Picasso, checking the identity of all guests before allowing each to proceed. Jake was on the cleared list. The one-minute review of Jake's credentials seemed like an eternity. He was so eager to meet Elizabeth. It was 3:00 a.m. when Jake gave the two rapid and two subsequent slow knocks on the door as instructed. Elizabeth looked through the peephole and opened the door.

"Thank you for coming to see me, Jake. I feel guilty taking you away from your family and a nice vacation, but selfishly I need you." Her eyelids drooped; Jake thought she looked exhausted. And beautiful. "I sent my husband back to London to recuperate from his trauma. He could have died. It's fortunate he left before the hotel concierge delivered photographs of you and me kissing. He would have been terribly hurt.

"Someone was following us," continued Elizabeth, "or one of us. Whoever delivered the photographs wanted a distraction for me in my work here. Jake, I was overjoyed to see you at breakfast," said Elizabeth. "I am very much to blame. A lot has happened since then. All said, I want you here with me."

"It's my fault, Elizabeth, for kissing you and wanting to touch you. I'm sorry," said Jake. "My wife and I had a terrible fight after the same package of photos arrived at our hotel room. She is pissed! I told her that you need assistance and that your husband is with you. Not sure she believes me, but she didn't object. Plus, I wanted very much to see you. You must know how glad I am to be with you."

Holding the hands of the woman who had been the object of his intense fantasy for two years, he inhaled the lavender scent of her perfume. He remembered it from London. He moved his hands down to the small of her back. He held the embrace, not wanting to rush what he had imagined so often.

He reached for her breasts. "Jake, I'm not sure I can tonight, with all that I have been through."

"Take your time, Elizabeth. I am here to support you in any way."

She placed her head on Jake's shoulder wrapping both arms around his waist.

"I feel so alone, Jake."

"I'm here."

A minute later she moved her hands to his thighs. He took a deep breath.

Jake slid his arms up Elizabeth's body, grasping both shoulders then softly cradling her neck. He reached under her hair and began kissing the side of her neck, her ears, then her eyelids, cheeks, and finally her parted lips. He could taste her cinnamon-colored lipstick, imagining it to be a secret aphrodisiac, casting a spell, which would trap him on a deserted island with her. If her song led him to crash among the rocks ending his career and marriage, so be it. The wreckage would be the fault of the beautiful siren. He was an innocent traveler forced by events onto the high seas of romance with no compass.

No words were exchanged. Elizabeth pulled him closer and pressed into his lips. Jake's whole body responded.

She grasped Jake's wrists and uttered a single word, "*Please*," and then guided his hands to her breasts and tensed nipples, turning her face up to kiss his lips, her mouth open on his.

Elizabeth took both of Jake's hands and pulled him to the bedroom. She fixed her eyes on his, moving backwards. She turned sideways, nudging him onto the bed, sliding on top of him. She whispered into his ear to wait on the bed until she called him.

After several minutes of anticipation, she called Jake, imploring him to join her right away. Jake walked into the bathroom to find her reclined in the Jacuzzi. He shed his clothes and climbed in behind her. She lay back against his chest, while he traced the soft contours of her breasts. He kissed the back of her neck; she rubbed his knees and thighs. He wrapped his arms around her in the warm water.

Jake caressed Elizabeth's abdomen and the tops of her thighs, tenderly pushing them apart. She kept her legs open, allowing Jake to explore and caress every part.

She stood up, turned around in the Jacuzzi to face him, sat down, and moved her hips closer to his.

Jake reached under her ass to give support, savoring the sensation. Flexing her knees up, Elizabeth spread her legs to allow his entrance. He knew she was supple and athletic but was amazed to see her lift both legs up onto his shoulders, feeling her calves high against his neck in an erotic display of remarkable agility.

Jake was in control, imploring time to suspend its immutable process. It took superhuman control not to thrust rapidly and reach an immediate release. Elizabeth extended her neck back and uttered his name in a low guttural sound.

In Jake's imagination the surface of the bath in the Jacuzzi suddenly appeared to have exploded with water blasting into the air, discharging with geyser force erupting with enormous turbulence built up under contained pressure. The eruption seemed to have begun with an ever-expanding emerald bubble, enlarging its base as though the captured thermal energy below forced it into a broadly rising torrent, eventually bursting the curved surface and filling the space above with wetness and steam. Primal sounds from the two lovers echoed in the bathroom as their bodies pulsed in unison.

Jake and Elizabeth embraced in the warm water. They held each other tightly for a long time, lingering in the afterglow of a magnificent fantasy finally realized. Jake wished to delay the inevitable return to baseline reality, and instead, basked in a motionless state of remarkable calmness, serenity, and surrender.

# XXIX

J ust after 1:00 p.m., confiding to his wife on the way to the airport in a taxi, his hearing still impaired, his leg pain abated, and his pride restored, Eduardo mentioned that he had gone to meet Ramón but was surprised and disappointed to find Pépe instead. The meeting began with the usual ritual: the two men had had a shot of whisky, after which Eduardo was invited to the back room to present his money for Ramón. Not wanting to offer details of the meeting in front of his daughter, Eduardo simply told his wife that things were arranged. The future was bright, and she had nothing to worry about.

In his own mind, Eduardo reviewed the events that had led to a last-minute flight. His new life, a new identity, and peace would begin in a few hours. Friends and relatives had agreed to create the new security he and his family needed. There would be newspaper articles about a family of three that simply disappeared. All family members would have new passports with aliases, not immediately but after arrival on the island.

The night before at Tio Pépe's, Eduardo had reached down into his soul and had summoned up the courage to be bold and powerful. He recognized that he was in a lifelong trap of extortion, having crossed Ramón one time. His life was racing to an abrupt end unless he took decisive steps. The well-being of his wife and daughter was at stake. If needed, he would die to save them. He had snorted diablito for a second time that day to bolster his courage and to stay on high alert. He felt committed. Courageous.

Eduardo had pointed to the back room in a respectful gesture to Pépe, allowing Eduardo to follow. Pépe agreed, probably because of the gun hidden in the desk drawer. When the door slammed closed behind them, Eduardo wasted no time. He pointed the revolver at Pépe and commanded him to sit at the computer. He held the gun at Pépe's left ear, telling him if he wanted to live, he should listen carefully.

Pépe remained calm in the face of Eduardo's threats and obliged. He opened the computer as instructed and went to the bank account file.

Eduardo instructed Pépe to enter the bank account password he and Ramón held, and to move the money to a secret account that Eduardo could access. Pépe was accommodating.

To his shock Eduardo saw that the account held almost two million euros!

With so much money at risk, he knew his future was tied to getting away with no witnesses. He ordered to Pépe to sit at a small metal chair and place his hands behind him. He placed ties over both wrists and then on both ankles in front of the chair. He then placed tape around Pepe's thighs, linking his body to the chair. Eduardo apologized for his actions. He wanted to offer no immediate threat to Pépe.

Pépe spoke softly, saying that no grudges would be held. "Just run with your money. This is easy money for us to acquire. We can also show you how to do this many times over. Ramón and I have often talked about a partnership with you." Eduardo doubted any such possibility.

Eduardo pulled out some tape, assuring Pépe that he just wanted to avoid any possible noise. He gave Pépe instructions, and Pépe nodded as a tremulous Eduardo placed tape across the captive's mouth. Then in a surprise move, he swiftly covered Pépe's nose. Watching Pépe raise his eyelids in disbelief, shaking his head as though pleading with him, he thought he saw a tear fall from each of Pépe's eyes.

Eduardo had been a quick student of Ramón and his history of deceptions. He placed the silencer on the gun and fired bullets into both of the bound man's knees. At times he thought he saw Ramón's face instead of Pépe's, and it gave him a sick pleasure.

Eduardo replaced the gun in his pocket, wrapped a small chain around Pépe's neck, fastening one end of it to an eye-hook in the wall. He placed a leather band above the chain which he would use to hang Pépe if the tape failed to suffocate him. Pépe moved his arms and wrists frantically in an attempt free himself, until all motion ceased. Without a whimper or a single inhalation his head slumped to one side.

Eduardo reached into his coat, this time to bring out a switchblade. He hated the symbol of fear, the tattooed eye, and wanted to cut it out.

He covered Pépe's head with a hood, hoping that Ramón would think it was a mob killing. He would later leave a note saying he fled the shop on seeing the chaotic scene in the back room.

Eduardo placed a call to the local police department. He announced that he was an anonymous tipster and wanted to report a possible homicide at Tio Pépe's. Two men had gotten into a fight and gone into the back room. All customers left the establishment quickly when gunshots were heard. He declined to say who he was, just that the police should know that Ramón had been arguing loudly with his partner in great anger and repeatedly threatening him. He then hung up the telephone.

He recounted the steps he had taken with the bartender and waiter, who had been conversing on stools in front of the bar. He wanted to leave no one behind who could give a description of him. He placed his hand in his pocket and approached them.

Free from his reverie, Eduardo looked affectionately at his wife in the taxi, "Lourdes. I love you so much, Te quiero a ti."

And he truly did. He was a caring husband and father, a man who knew best how to protect his family. Their future would be wonderful.

# XXX

Jake was delighted to be in Elizabeth's company, even if mostly for a business wrap-up. Elizabeth thanked Jake and Chris for meeting her early for coffee at the office of Toni Palacios. She introduced Toni and Javier. Toni sat tall at the table, but Javier paced around the group. Two other security men were having breakfast across the hall at an adjoining office. New questions prompted the meeting, summarizing the events of the night before at Tio Pépe's, yet avoiding some of the gruesome details.

"Thank you, doctors, for your help. Your analysis of the hospitalized patients was critical. It led us to the fact that the non-injured patients all were linked to some kind of medical device," noted Toni. "That brought us to the reluctant conclusion that the devices' programs had been hacked. But there is more. Following your lead, our cyber security team has investigated the computer programs that keep these devices working. The surprise came next, and Elizabeth's husband experienced it first hand when the MRI machine stopped working."

"The forensic cyber team," Javier said, "discovered that the network supporting the devices had been briefly hacked. It was short-lived but enough time for the malware to appear dysfunctional, but function of the malware was fully restored without being recognized."

"How do your cyber experts explain that?" asked Jake.

Javier looked concerned. "It means the hackers could enter and leave the program at will. They didn't just overwhelm and destroy the program. They created their own new access, a unique pathway into the programming by finding an opening, what we call a *trap door* in cyber terms."

Javier reviewed what the cyber experts had reported to Toni and him earlier. The level of sophistication was novel and complex. First, the hackers used access ports typically allowed by firewalls with some looking like a Windows messenger with embedded malware. "You might think of the effort as one to blend the legitimate traffic with malware traffic so as to avoid detection, a disguise of sorts," said Javier. "The hackers used interesting subject lines for the spear-phishing emails to attract and lure potential targets into opening the malicious attachments.

"A key to the malware is what is called a RAT or remote access tool, which allows the hacker to be at a great distance from the hacked computers," Javier explained. "In this case, even the communication between the compromised computers and the RAT controllers was encrypted, another effort to evade or slow down detection. When delivering malicious payloads, hackers use encryption algorithms with very advanced obfuscation methods," he said.

Toni added the possibility that international cyber criminals could be involved. "An organization based in Sweden called *Blackshades* developed sophisticated RATs and sold thousands of copies to cyber terrorists worldwide in 2010. A few years after, using a program called *Spreaders*, Blackshades' malware could remotely spread to other computers. It was estimated in 2014 that over a half a million computers had been compromised, he added.

"All said," concluded Javier, "this is a remarkably sophisticated evolution of a remote-access tool designed for malicious harm, one never seen previously."

Elizabeth interrupted, "What we worry most about now is what this may imply. What is the goal of such malware? Why would these people with underlying medical devices be targeted? Is there more coming?"

Toni nodded. "What we know is that some of the visiting dignitaries have medical devices, and they would be especially vulnerable. They may be a real target, and the initial terror event with the diversion of an explosion was only a test. The failure of large radiology equipment and other medical technology failings in so many hospitals leads our cyber guys to think that they may have targeted our entire national health care system. Two hospitals have reported hacking of their operating room schedules. There may be more."

Cracking his knuckles and still pacing, Javier went on. "Our experts discovered a unique hacking approach to the trap door, one not seen before. Like many, the door can be accessed remotely, but this one is amazingly rapid and can be duplicated in several locations in the program. It is remarkably difficult to repair, thus offering a redundancy of options in case one or more would be discovered and deleted."

"Imagine the Trojan horse," said Elizabeth, "with four entrances to secret hiding places of warriors, so that even if one were discovered, the others would remain available. The people of Troy would be in for a complete surprise as they relaxed in the knowledge that they had discovered a vulnerable issue and neutralized it.

"Your medical knowledge and epidemiological work helped immensely and may have saved the lives of our visiting states persons," said Elizabeth, looking at Jake with a brief smile. Jake was pleased with this compliment, nodding thanks. "You gave the cyber analysts early warning, which led to their recognizing a frightening capability. Thank you." Elizabeth's last two words were said very tenderly, but to Jake she appeared weary, pale, and distant. For a brief moment he knew that he was more interested in his relationship with Elizabeth than in cyber terror.

"The new question," said Toni, "relates to whether or not a new target is at risk with this sophisticated malware. Of course it could be applied to other programs affecting the infrastructure of Spain and perhaps other countries. We still would like you doctors to imagine what might be at risk in the medical population while we explore alternatives."

Jake offered the grim possibility that entire hospital network computer systems could be at risk. He was quite fatigued and looked to Chris for confirmation.

"It would be disastrous for the medical system," said Chris. "There are only four or five commercial programs purchased by most hospitals in the U.K. and the U.S., though some hospitals have home-grown systems that are stand alone or enhancements to the commercial product."

Trying to be useful, Jake asked the group to imagine no functioning registration system for patients, no patient portals, no operating room schedules on-line, or on-line pharmacy ordering. No automatic disinfection or sterilization system, no reliable labs. "Imagine the medical world with everything back to hand-written notes. For reliability we would abandon all automation, and all testing and treatment would rely on methodology that is 15 to 30 years old!" He recalled his medical training when all students learned to do their own blood counts on patients, examine urine specimens under the microscope for white cells, and do the Gram stain on sputum specimens to look for specific bacteria-causing pneumonia. The current crop of doctors wouldn't be prepared.

"Jake and Chris," said Elizabeth, "I suppose you're ready to leave all of this intrigue, and I can't blame you. You've been a great help, and we're grateful. Hopefully, you'll have a less eventful end to your holiday in London."

"Yes, Elizabeth," said Chris, "our families are uncomfortable and look forward to some quiet time at home, full of relaxation and free of worry."

"Please thank your children for their lead," Elizabeth said. "The dead man we discovered as a result of their observations was Pépe, thought to be a lesser player in this intrigue. The current whereabouts of his partner, Ramón, is unknown. What we know so far is Ramón is a violent man with ties to the underworld in several countries, and we suspect him to have helped some terrorists in the past.

"For now I believe Ramón was the disguised waiter who almost killed my husband and fled before Diana Kontos arrived. Their relationship is a focus of our attention.

"And who is the couple you two doctors saw at the beach? Why was one of them possibly tied to a terrorist group in Corsica? None of this is clear at this time."

Pointing to the hallway, Elizabeth asked Jake if she could ask him a clinical question related to her husband's health. Without expression Jake followed her down a long hallway to a smaller room. He wanted more time with her, no matter where or when.

"Jake, I haven't had a lot of sleep, so my emotions may be frayed. I'm so fond of you and enjoyed last night immensely. But it was a mistake. I have obligations and realize I have to move on. I am committed to my husband and children and love all of them. I'm sure you can understand or at least I hope so."

Jake dismissed this possibility. He couldn't understand. He did not want to give up, "Can we talk about this later when we've caught up with sleep and this terror business is all over?"

"No, Jake, I'm serious. I want us both to preserve our marriages."

They squeezed each other's hands and returned to the others. All were again seated at the table. Jake failed to mention that Deb had again opened up the package of photos delivered to the hotel room and suggested that this was the beginning of the end for them. She said she would not bring this up on the trip and would not mention anything to Mary or the children at this time.

Staring blankly into space, Jake recalled the first time he met Elizabeth, so stunning in her pinstriped suit. Now it was all over. And maybe worse, he thought, replaying Deb's anger. "Did you have fun with this woman?" Deb had asked, tossing the photo of the embrace. "And around her neck she had the same fucking necklace you gave to me! You bastard!"

"Deb, I did hug her and am fond of her, but I love you and the children. She is committed to her husband and children. The local investigators want Chris and me to have a 30-minute meeting over coffee in a few hours. They have a few questions more. Then it is over. We leave for the airport to London. I'll do whatever is needed to show you I want us to remain together."

Deb was unmoved. "Jake, back in Palo Alto we need to discuss where we are in our relationship. I'm serious." With that statement she left for the bedroom, slamming the door shut. Jake stayed in the TV room alone and completed his packing followed by a shower and shave. Disorientation and a feeling of dizziness overwhelmed him. His world was unraveling. He desperately wanted the security of his family, but he also wanted more of Elizabeth. Both were in jeopardy. He had work to do.

Jake looked up from his reverie at the table in Toni's office. Javier and Chris talked intensely to each other. Toni Palacious excused himself, announcing he was taking a call from the police station. He returned with a concerned look. "Two planes with foreign dignitaries from the UK and France, respectively, have had a modest change in schedule. Each will arrive one hour earlier. These two men rely on medical devices and are especially vulnerable. We need to accelerate our welcoming preparations at once." He and Javier left the room.

Jake's expression signaled his confusion, as he and Elizabeth walked together down a hallway. "Elizabeth, we can work this out, even if oceans apart and with completely different professional responsibilities. I'm not sure how, but I must have more of you," he whispered softly.

Elizabeth took a deep breath. "Jake, in our times together, I am totally enamored with you, too. But each time I had to move on, as did you. Please try to see this reality. If you do, I'll admire you greatly. If you cannot, I'll remind you that you are married. So am I."

She added: "I need to catch Diana Kontos! That's my focus, Jake, my only focus."

# XXXI

L istening intensely to an early morning newscaster discuss the horrifying details surrounding three men killed at Tio Pépe's, Ramón, unshaven with puffy eyes and a sense of heaviness and fatigue, tried to imagine what went down. It looked like gangland revenge, but he knew most of the bandas' Jefes. He had not created any obvious enemies. Could Pépe possibly have created a problem unknown to him? So what would be the motive anyway? He took another shot of whiskey, his fifth or sixth in a row.

Did MI-5 raid the shop in wanton fashion, killing everyone in sight, hoping to nail him? Of course MI-5 would want to hide the killing of Agent Foster's husband, so it was not surprising that no reports surfaced on TV. That's not how they operate.

Surely that pudgy wimp Eduardo couldn't pull this off without some underground friends. And who in hell would work for the little shit anyway? Ramón thought it prudent to wait for further details from the police. In the meantime, he'd contact some of the more prominent gang leaders for information, ready to apologize if he sensed some inadvertent offense. He'd also call Eduardo just to be complete. After all, he enjoyed intimidating the simple asshole. Might be a boost on this gloomy day.

The windowless back room of the bodega where he was holed up contained only a narrow cot and small television. The owner, a trusted businessman, sold wine and tapas and dealt in the local trade of marijuana. He had invited Ramón to "stay as long as he needed," after Ramón asked for help. Having completed a few drug sales on the opposite side of Barcelona, Ramón was listening to the car radio when he learned of the police raid on his return on back roads in the cloak of night. That is when he contacted his colleague Francisco, who he could intimidate, if necessary, to secure a hiding place.

First things first, thought Ramón. He'd call the bank to be sure the account was intact. Maybe the hit was for money. It was already 10 a.m. Using Francisco's landline to dial the direct business number of Wil Cabezudo, Ramón introduced himself as the man Wil had met the day before.

Señor Cabezudo stunned Ramón with the news. "Our records show that you transferred the money remotely to a bank in Majorca the evening before last," he said. The man told him all security questions had been answered within the defined response time, and the secure password was entered correctly the first time without delay.

"Chingada!" screamed Ramón. How in the fuck did that happen? Only Pépe and he knew the computer password and sign on. He slammed the phone down.

Whoever killed Pépe must have forced him to move the account. That meant gang violence was the most likely possible motive, surely not the work of MI-5. But how did the gang members know the large size of the account? Was there a lack of security at the bank? And why would the gangs target his partner anyway?

It remained a remote possibility that Eduardo was involved. He was supposed to bring money yesterday, but Ramón had asked Pépe instead to meet with him when he needed to have a last-minute meeting on the other side of Barcelona. But who would Eduardo get to help him? And he would have no idea how much cash was in the account. Pépe would have nailed Eduardo to the wall if Eduardo threatened him in any way. Impossible!

Ramón called Eduardo's cell phone. An automated response announced that the "service was discontinued." Not a big surprise by itself. Problems happen with cell phones. Ramón tried his home phone, and the same message was delivered. Ramón punched a hole in the thin wall board of the enclosed room. A local gang member had knocked off his partner. Somehow Eduardo must have been involved and was advised to leave town. Eduardo and his accomplices had to die and suffer slowly and painfully. He obviously didn't get the message the last time. He should have killed that pudgy prick in the back room.

Something continued to nag at him. The more he thought about it, the transfer of money to Majorca made it less likely that it was a local gang.

He made calls to three jefes. He wanted to find out if the most prominent bosses in Barcelona harbored any anger toward Pépe or himself. If so, he would do whatever was needed to repair any ill feelings. Immediately.

Each responded in a similar way. No. In fact, no one had any problems with him or his associate and all had full respect for both. Importantly, no one had asked for their gang's help in committing such a violent hit. Each also expressed regret for his loss and wished him luck. They seemed genuinely sorry that his partner had died at the hands of a very angry person, possibly a deranged psychopath.

That was reassuring, thought Ramón. If it wasn't MI-5 and most likely not a gang killing, it might be a random act by a crazy person or an execution by Eduardo with help from a hired killer. His phones didn't work, and that was no coincidence. Where would Eduardo hide?

On a hunch, he telephoned the Barcelona airport and learned that two flights were scheduled to go to Majorca later that day. He called both airlines.

He stated that he was a last-minute traveler and was hoping to sit near his close friend, Señor Eduardo Felice. Were such seats still available before he committed to the flight? The first carrier said that no one by the name Felice was booked. Ramón thanked the agent and hung up. The youthful agent at the second carrier was reluctant to give out any information. She was willing to bend the rules, however, when Ramón explained that his childhood friend had a terminal disease with only days remaining. He had hoped to comfort him and help his family cope in this time of grief. "I simply wanted to help him during his last days on earth."

"Señor Felice, his wife, and daughter will be on the 4 p.m. flight," she reported. "Should I book your ticket as well? I regret that the closest seat available is three rows away, but I'm sure someone will be willing to switch seats during the boarding process."

"Yes, of course. That's perfect. I'll surprise him at the airport. And please, for his health, don't say anything about this call. This is so important. I want only for his life to be filled with peace, a quiet calm before he leaves us for a better place."

Ramón showered, shaved, and dyed his hair completely gray. He added a grayish white mustache and put on dark glasses and a suit borrowed from Francisco. He reviewed a list of options for dealing with Eduardo. Each involved the element of surprise and an uncomfortable ending. He wanted Eduardo to look directly into his eyes. It would be a face-to-face encounter that would terrify that fucker beyond his wildest fears.

# XXXII

At 5 a.m., Kleïs was fixated on the TV announcer reporting lurid details of the death of one of the proprietors of Tio Pépe's. The reporter highlighted the supposition that the man had been savagely murdered in a gangland-style execution. The authorities were looking for his partner, a man named Ramón Contreras, describing him only as a person of interest. If anyone had information, they should not attempt to approach him but should call the authorities at the number on the screen.

Sipping coffee in bed, Kleïs wondered who could have killed Pépe. Did Ramón kill him and take all the money? If so, where could Ramón be now? Perhaps greed led to Pépe's death. But why so brutal a killing? She looked at Diana and raised the questions out loud.

"Kleïs, I'm eager to find Ramón and hope to be ahead of the authorities or the gang that tortured Pépe. I don't want him in a comfortable jail," said Diana. "I want him to taste vengeance."

The big story just breaking was the loss of power involving radiology and some laboratory equipment at area hospitals and the desperate moves by medical personnel to help patients with life-supporting devices that now were malfunctioning. Some type of cyber terror was suspected, though no one could recall seeing this manner of malware before.

"Kleïs, they have no concept of cyber terror!" exclaimed Diana, kissing Kleïs's cheek. "Your skills are beyond anything they can imagine. But soon they will understand."

With reporters on site at four area medical centers, the city was beginning to panic. Numerous citizens were interviewed, many of whom had friends or relatives in the hospital. They asked questions more than they made comments. How soon would the government be able to squelch this kind of threat? Was more coming? What were the terrorists' objectives and who were they? Politicians who had been interviewed began pointing fingers at each other in divisive terms. Right-wing politicians blamed the soft crime policies of liberal lawmakers. They had been warned of cyber terror and the need for funding to control this type of threat for years. Liberals claimed their critics were too quick to judge, since the facts were still unclear. They suggested that extreme right-wing fanatics should be considered behind it all.

"Just a matter of time," said Kleïs, "before people demand change."

The news commentators continued to report on the lurid murders. Government officials were having high-level discussions with law enforcement and security experts to develop appropriate responses. All were hesitant to speculate on who might be behind the terror or their eventual goals. Press meetings would be held any time new facts were clarified and at the end of the working day. While asking people to be alert, each government spokesperson encouraged citizens to be extra vigilant but also proclaimed there was no need to panic. The government had its arms around the problem. On-the-street interviews expressed generally held doubts that a solution was near.

Kleïs continued editing a draft of a demand document she was planning to deliver electronically to *El Pais,* the leading national newspaper in Spain. The introduction would be clear and concise with details below: *ETA prisoners will be released immediately, and the country has one month to declare a separate Basque state. More devastating malware will be released if demands are not met, and the authorities must agree publicly in forty-eight hours.*

Panos would send an email afterwards to *Le Monde* in Paris taking credit for the malware and demanding a free state of Corsica. The malfunctioning of medical devices and the loss of power at hospitals in Paris would begin in twenty-four hours. If French citizens wanted to see the future, they need to look no farther than their neighbors in Spain. Panos did not expect the French government to respond to this threat. A reaction would come but only after the malware was activated. It was so stupid to delay an inevitable response when the request was so insignificant to France. "It would be delicious to watch the French citizens lose confidence in their government," said Kleïs. The third and prime target, Israel, was always high in her mind.

In the ecstasy of all that had happened, she and Diana had made love for an hour before turning on the television news station. Finding Ramón remained an imminent key goal, but each had an unusual optimism as though the Fates were guiding their course. They hated Ramón also for creating a distraction in their plans. Was there no loyalty left in the world? No honor? Did Ramón have any idea that betrayal was the birth of vendettas? Did he learn nothing from the culture of Corsica?

Diana opened an email that just arrived. The message from the owner of a small bodega offered special hope. "This is wonderful news!" Diana whispered loudly, patting the bed three times in excitement. It was Francisco, the man who had introduced Kleïs and Diana at the

International Days of Corte in Corsica. Both women thought that destiny had tied the three together in a special bond, and all three vowed to stay in touch. Generally they had exchanged calls or emails every month, using code to give updates on their "projects." Both women knew that Francisco had been aware of the local partnership of Diana with Ramón. They told him not to turn his back on Ramón. He is unpredictable but always dangerous.

Diana read his own admonition out loud: *you too must be cautious, be discreet.* Passing the phone to Kleïs, Diana pointed to the final sentence in the proprietor's note. Ramón had mentioned a possible killer named Eduardo, now bound for the airport for an afternoon flight to Majorca. Apparently the flight was scheduled for late afternoon. No more details had been given to him.

Both women were elated with the information, recognizing that a debt had to be paid, that deception was among the worst of all offences, honor was at stake, and the time was near to avenge the wrong. "What happened to chivalry? Did Ramón think we would turn the other cheek? Does that small-minded bastard underestimate me so much?" Diana asked in a gravelly tone, her face reddening with fury.

Thanks to Francisco's information, Diana and Kleïs had a new and compelling reason to be at the airport, to meet Ramón and end his time on earth. They would be in disguise, and illusion would be their close ally in the fatal encounter.

Kleïs flipped the sheets to the side, exposing the nude body of her attractive lover. Diana joined her in the shower, where they soaped each other's skin and rubbed shampoo in each other's hair. The warm waters rained down on them, washing away the passion of the earlier hours. Kleïs stood behind Diana, pressing against her buttocks, embracing her breasts, and whispering lines from Sappho.

Drying off with peach-colored towels, they discussed Ramón. Diana had plans for the day and needed to prepare. Both knew how violent, how ruthless he could be. They needed to focus on caution and the element of surprise, exploit his key vulnerability, then move on to the goals they had prepared for over the last year. They would make a stop on the way to the airport.

Diana couldn't clear her mind of Ramón's betrayal. Her anger was linked to his foiled attempt to have her captured by the hotel security team. He was not only a liar but had also caused much distraction. And he stole money, the funds for needy Palestinians.

Some men abuse everyone around them, then wonder why the abused become their nemeses. A traitor always has to suffer, thought Kleïs. He wouldn't be expecting her at the airport, but he would soon understand the meaning of "Greeks bearing gifts."

# XXXIII

D iana's father walked purposely towards the spot where he was to meet his daughter. It was long overdue, he thought. Diana had not seen her father for an extended visit for over a year when he had arrived unexpectedly in a small town on the West Bank to meet his grandson for the first time. It was the summer of 2014, when Israel invaded Gaza and killed off so many Palestinians. There were spontaneous, angry demonstrations in the West Bank protesting the deaths of Palestinian civilians, and Amer had worried for Diana's safety.

Amer recalled the day he met Jawhara, Diana's mother, in a Lebanese refugee camp. He was a young member of *Fedayeen*, an angry group of men determined to avenge the loss of their homes to the Zionists. Amer, with help of his colleagues, arranged for a clandestine escape of Jawhara and Diana's grandmother, Rana, on an Egyptian cargo plane to Cairo and then to Athens. Amer and Jawhara married a few years afterwards. It was in Athens that Diana and Sasha listened nightly as small children and later as young teens to their grandmother's stories about the injustices the family had suffered and the need to avenge.

He was so proud of his daughter and grandson. He had never imagined the bond could be so strong between a man and his grandchild. He remained with them for two weeks, reading stories to the boy, carrying him on his shoulders, speaking in Arabic and Greek, offering the best oral traditions of the family's history. He knew his grandson would understand little of what he said, but over time he would repeat the messages about struggle, pride, perseverance, honor, and family.

After that visit, Amer and Diana had often spoken on the phone, had enjoyed brief afternoon visits, and used encrypted emails to remain in contact. Still sought by the British authorities and Interpol, Amer was careful to travel on one of several counterfeit passports whenever he left Palestine. While there, he remained most of the time in Hebron, helping secure funds to support their current independence efforts from Israel. This was not an older man's job, he reflected. Perhaps it was time to relinquish the tasks to a younger colleague.

He knew of Diana's relationship with Kleïs and asked her what was she like, what characteristics attracted her? What interests did they share? Any in which they were discordant? Admiring a photo of the two sent by email, he called to see if he, Diana and Kleïs could meet, even for thirty minutes while he was in Barcelona. It was so convenient they were both to be in Spain at the same time working on projects with Panos.

When he contacted Diana, she hesitated. She told him that her time was tight but perhaps they could meet for coffee and he could meet Kleïs. She mentioned a small cafe just off the airport road as a possible meeting venue, or the airport itself, since she had some business there.

He suggested one of the airport coffee shops. They would meet in late morning, plenty of time to talk.

At 11 a.m. Diana and her father embraced each other, both with eyes welling from the unspoken deep love and regret. It was palpable to Amer how much his daughter loved him. He admired her for her devotion to a shared commitment: the plight of the displaced Palestinians, their loss of civil rights, their pent-up frustrations, their dependence on an occupying force for travel, jobs, food on the table, electricity. He knew that she worked tirelessly and hoped that eventually both pride and property would one day be restored in an independent Palestinian state.

Diana told her father that he was still a handsome man and appeared much younger than his eighty-four years. He reached over to hug her and he said softly, "Thank you."

Amer turned to Kleïs and took her hand. He looked with special scrutiny over her face. "It is a pleasure to meet you at long last. My name is Amer."

Securing a high-back booth, screened from the general crowd, all three sat down and ordered cappuccino. Amer began with news of Diana's mother living near Athens and still in generally good health, but sometimes complaining of forgetfulness and worrying that her mind is fading. She was stiff all over, especially in the mornings. Amer said he made great efforts to see and comfort his wife, but authorities made it difficult even to capture a few minutes together.

Father and daughter exchanged the persistent sad feelings over the loss of Sasha. Neither could talk about her easily, the burden too heavy, the memory etched too raw.

Amer redirected conversation to the good news. Diana's son, Achilles, was doing well and possessed a strong vocabulary for a boy of two.

"I miss him," said Diana, a soft gravel in her voice.

Amer turned to Kleïs and inquired about her family, her upbringing, and her chance meeting with Diana. He knew Crete well, he said, and thought that her upbringing was in a special place on this earth, the cradle of civilization. His mind traveled for a moment to the special countries on both sides of the Mediterranean, as well as the islands within the sea, places he loved and had frequented in his efforts to garner support for Palestine.

Kleïs was absolutely astonished and charmed by this man who knew her village so well, even the café where her mother and father had met. Amer said he knew her father quite well, of course, and he was almost positive that he had met her mother on one of his stays on the island.

To Diana's surprise he said that when Diana and Sasha were two years old, he took them to Crete while on a trip from Athens. Diana's mother was off visiting an ill uncle. Though they had met earlier, it was on that visit that he again met Kleïs' father. Diana had no recollection of this visit at all, thinking again that her father worked in strange fashion, conspiring to shrink the world at times. "We met a year later on the island of Mykonos," said Amer.

Finishing up his coffee, Diana's father asked if either woman needed money. He could easily help. Both responded they were fine and perhaps by the end of the day, one way or another, they would recoup some stolen funds useful for their project in Palestine.

Not seeking to inquire about this, Amer said he was grateful to have gotten together. He had arranged to transact business nearby and would be at the airport before returning to Palestine via private jet. He stood up to leave. He gave each woman a warm embrace and started to walk away, then hesitated.

"I almost forgot, Diana, I have something for you, something you might share with Kleïs." He passed a sealed envelope onto the table. He turned and walked away, disappearing into the faceless crowd of frenetic travelers.

The women sat down to finish their coffee and rehearse their plans. Kleïs expressed her pleasure at meeting Diana's father. Both were curious about the envelope. Diana reached over to break the seal, and found inside a piece of white paper that wrapped around an old black and white photograph.

Three young girls at the edge of the sea were holding hands, posing for the unknown photographer. Two were obviously twins, about three or four years old, and the third, probably five years old.

"Look, Kleïs, this is a childhood photo of my sister Sasha and me. I have no idea who we were playing with, and I don't even recognize the area. I can't even recall the visit to the beach. This is so special to have a picture of my sister, one reminding me of our childhood, now the oldest photo I have of her."

On the back of the picture the inscription simply read: *My three daughters – on Mykonos*. Amer.

Kleïs examined the photo and froze. She couldn't explain her feelings. Above all it was so confusing. She was the third girl in the photo.

# XXXIV

F rom two cars away Elizabeth observed Jake, Chris, and their families enter a van with security officers on board to escort the group to the airport. To her eyes Jake and his wife seemed stressed. Chris and his wife appeared to be more comfortable, and the children quite excited. Elizabeth was aware that the two families had booked a 4:15 p.m. flight to London and seemed grateful for the extra precautions. They were pleased to leave for the airport hours before the scheduled departure and happy to travel to a safer city for now. The driver and front seat passenger were armed Spanish policemen. A car with two other agents would follow the van to the airport. Elizabeth chose not to meet the members of the two families.

Javier and Toni, in combat fatigues with three other similarly clad officers, would be making their way to the airport in a bullet-proof riot wagon to assist arriving dignitaries. Elizabeth was in a civilian outfit, a blue pantsuit, with a weapon in her jacket pocket. They would be escorting them expeditiously through an elite version of customs and subsequently to a secured building on the outskirts of Barcelona. Sitting in the van, the team discussed current threats and responses and computer hackers in general.

"Thanks to Jake's epidemiological work, the cyber counter-terror team was alerted several hours before the power went out in all the city's hospitals. Cyber team members, including Batman and Robin, reported they might be able to remove the malware in about 12 hours, a deadline which is quickly approaching," said Elizabeth.

"Meanwhile the city is erupting in chaos," said Toni. All doctors had been summoned to clinics and hospitals, many military physicians being flown in just in case the situation deteriorated even more. Javier said patients were panicked about their blood sugar levels, cardiac rhythm problems, x-ray needs. People with friends and relatives in ICUs were flocking to hospitals to be sure all their loved ones were still alive and safe. "So far, 48 deaths had been attributed to malfunctioning equipment, but most authorities said the true number might reach 200," Toni noted. Some were packing clothes and making arrangements to drive out of cities to smaller rural villages. The radio was releasing a list of smaller hospitals still using manual systems, thus likely to be safe from their more modern, computerized counterparts. Since word got out that financial institutions were at risk, banks were being inundated with patrons withdrawing funds.

"I heard a report," said Javier, "all area medical, nursing, and pharmacy students have been assigned to one of several area hospitals. They were told to bring toiletries and plan to spend several days at the hospitals."

"People have talked about cyber terror for years, Javier, but no one has truly planned for it," Elizabeth said. "Still fewer have considered the social consequences. We are witnessing that now. This is more than a wakeup call for law enforcement and security."

"Agreed, Elizabeth," responded Javier, "and fewer still have worked on medical device hacking or have developed a clear response plan. We're writing the book now."

"All the governments in the free world are getting stunned with this one," exclaimed Toni. "Our colleagues should have moved more quickly when it became apparent that a new industry had evolved, involving hacking and notifying governments and private industry that flaws in computer codes had been discovered and could be remedied for a price. This was a tolerated kind of cyber ransom. These are just the greedy bastards, hacking for money, but they coincidentally open up doors for the really bad guys."

Toni recalled that two Italian hackers on Malta had clients including the National Security Agency, Microsoft, and Apple. Countries including the U.S., Israel, and Britain were willing customers of similar hackers. Once commercial hackers discovered a flaw, the clock started for other global hackers with more malicious intent to discover it. The time between the date the cyber ransom was initiated and the date when the secondary and more malicious hackers discovered the flaw was referred to as *zero days* — the period within which the flaw needed to be repaired before another hacker broke in. By the time industry received the news, high stakes blackmail was demanded and proprietary information was in jeopardy. It was the cost of business now. Most people had no idea that this was going on, but as customers and citizens, they were paying for it.

"Some countries," explained Toni, "are outbidding industry, thus allowing access to proprietary secrets. It's believed that the success of the U.S. and Israel in attacking Iran's nuclear enrichment program in 2010 with the *Stuxnet* worm was a byproduct of such bidding," he said.

"The problem of course," emphasized Javier, "is that such success is quite temporary, and even if a novel hacking approach is used, the secret is available for the next hacker, who could sell it or employ it for personal benefit. It's impossible to hide the latest method of cyber terror."

"The commercial hacking business is very lucrative," continued Javier. "The demand has created a gold rush, a large enough global enterprise that, believe it or not, now supports brokers who connect buyers and sellers, just like the stock market. Clearly it's blackmail, but not paying could leave a business with an insecure project or a country in great jeopardy."

"The dignitaries are expected to arrive between 3:30 and 5 p.m., Elizabeth," Toni said, looking at notes on his iPhone. "The sooner we can get them to our heavily secured meeting venue, the better. We have asked the two VIPs with medical devices to reprogram each with a new platform unaffected by what may be used here. Both have complied. Hopefully, that will be enough."

Elizabeth reviewed notifications from London confirming the sighting of Diana Kontos in Casablanca, suggesting that Jake and Chris really did see her on the Icarian beach with a person linked to Corsica. A violent organization from Corsica was surfacing as the group behind the current cyber-attack.

Still focused on her phone, Elizabeth began reading the next notification out loud. A young Interpol agent had been found murdered in Casablanca, apparently soon after sighting Diana Kontos there. Her body was located in an abandoned house on the outskirts of the city. She was highly intelligent, spoke six languages, and was one of the most promising in her cohort of young agents. She was to be married in three months.

Grim details were emerging, filling in the missing pieces. Was there a relationship between Diana Kontos, a person in Corsica, and the proprietors of Tio Pépe's? If so, what were the ties? And who killed one of them so violently?

"We're happy your husband avoided still more pain or worse," said Toni. "How is he doing in London?"

"Thank you, he's sore all over but safe and otherwise comfortable. He feels guilty for coming with me on assignment but grateful to be alive. Our boys are looking after him," responded Elizabeth. "I'm also grateful for the good news."

"In the meantime," continued Toni, "we have agents following up leads of both owners of Tio Pépe's, and all staff at the hotel where you are staying. After all, someone must have helped Ramón. We're also looking at all people linked to any cyber crimes. We are essentially going door to door in some neighborhoods.

"Elizabeth, I think we are prepared and unlikely to be caught off guard. We're grateful for your help and the link to Diana Kontos. We'll will catch her, I assure you, and we'll do it together so that you have the satisfaction of her capture at last. We can focus on that aspect of our job after our day at the airport. I do appreciate your willingness to help us there. With all the security and rapid transit of dignitaries, I expect a quiet day today. It should be quite uneventful, but my mantra is never let our guard down."

Elizabeth nodded, looking forward to the adrenaline rush of chasing the fugitives. Downtime never satisfied her.

# XXXV

I n the corner of an airport bar Panos greeted Amer and led him to seats out of sight of the other customers, who were readying themselves for flight by downing anxiety-numbing drinks. Money from friends of Palestine would be transferred to secure accounts for use by those sympathetic to Corsica's desire for independence. The debt would be repaid at a future time when assets from Corsica's elite rebels could help the Palestinian cause.

In their embrace, Panos recalled the years of an improbable friendship with Amer, over six decades now, born in part from their common political interests but more importantly from personal family interests. In the late 1940s, undercover agents of the newly formed country of Israel had trailed Amer to Crete. Labeled a key terrorist by the Zionists, the youthful teenager Amer was continually on the run. In Crete, a sympathetic Panos hid him in his attic for four weeks.

Still lost in thought, Panos remembered the years after he and his wife were married. His sweetheart was one of six and wanted a large family. They had been trying to conceive when he underwent the evaluation.

On a sunny afternoon in early fall, Panos walked to Syntagma Square in central Athens, sat down at an outdoor café table for two, and ordered a small glass of ouzo. He added water and ice, stared at the cloudy white liquid and waited. The waiter brought a small white plate with olives, sardines, and feta, but Panos neither drank nor ate, too despondent to appreciate the food and aperitif.

Forty-five minutes later, a smiling Amer approached the table, slapped Panos' shoulder, and sat down. Amer thanked him for inviting him to meet and apologized for his delay in arriving. His eyes met Panos' wan expression, and he knew something serious was disturbing his friend.

"I'm not feeling well, Amer, and I have a very unusual request."

"Of course, Panos, how can I help?"

Over the next hour Panos explained his love for Ana, her need to have children, and his own inability to produce children. A month-long series of tests had led to an unfortunate conclusion: it was unlikely that Panos could father children. His sperm count was very low. There was another option for him, the lead physician had offered. A sperm donor could be used; the method was popular and successful using both known and anonymous donors. The doctor hoped Panos would find a donor close to him.

"That is why I asked you to join me, Amer. You are a dear friend, so special and so discreet. I would like you to be a donor for a child that I would raise." He paused to allow Amer to process this proposal. "I know it is a huge issue for you to consider."

Observing Amer's face, Panos recognized that Amer was conflicted. He imagined his friend's questions. What ethical storm are you sailing into? How would you relate to a future child? Could you visit the child and should he be present on special occasions or special holidays? Whom would you tell this to? What would be the long-term obligations to a child from a sperm donor? Amer continued sipping the ouzo as though allowing some time to think, to pause to try to reflect.

A moment later Amer put his glass down. "I will help you, my friend." He knew that he was alive because of the courage of his friend. Could he visit the family on occasion, he had asked. Panos agreed quickly.

Amer visited Crete with his own twin daughters only once when they were small children and only on rare occasions later by himself. He and Amer had a father's weekend in Mykonos a year later. He offered money frequently, which Panos always declined. Panos retained a strong friendship with Amer, who seemed to hold a fondness for Crete and for checking in on Kleïs.

Over the years, the two men and Ana were the only ones to know of the relationship between Kleïs and Diana. They had only recently agreed that since chance had brought the young women together, they should know the truth. Amer had agreed to open that door.

More recently, both friends had wrestled with how much they should reveal to the daughters at one time and how the revelation might affect their personal relationship. After some discussion they concluded that just announcing the fundamental relationship was a wise first step. After the two women had come to grips with the key issues, the story behind the request decades ago, based on the love between Panos and Ana, could be seen in the most accurate and affectionate perspective. It was at that moment that Amer suggested presenting the two with the photograph of the twins with Kleïs, a precious memento that Amer had carried in his wallet for over forty years.

At the airport bar they each ordered a small sherry and softly described their next goals. With luck, the prime minister of France would be eliminated on this visit to Barcelona with the cyber-attack on his medical device, and agents in Paris were already in place to contact the president of France. With such high-profile targets, the French government would be wrestling with the simple demand to free Corsica. But if more persuasion was needed after the first wave of medical device malfunctions reached the shores of France, more infrastructures would be the next targets.

Panos tipped his glass to Amer. Amer returned the gesture. It was a salute to their long friendship and plans. They were distant supporters of the daughters' goals.

"It's been a long time coming," noted Panos.

"The prime minister of Israel is next, my friend," whispered Amer. "But we hope to have him make a foolish preemptive strike on Iran, destroying his relationship with America before he is eliminated."

Amer lifted his small glass as a toast to Panos, one of a handful of friends he completely trusted. "In my 9th decade now, Panos, each day is a treasure. One never knows when the sun will cease to offer its light on life's path. I like to think that my efforts have made a difference, that the oppressed have been offered some hope at times.

"I don't believe in the unexamined life. I recognize that important tradeoffs were made in my time, especially those affecting my family." A slight rasp took command of his voice, and Amer swallowed a sip of the aperitif before continuing.

"I like to think that I have been witness to reality, responding nobly, not seeing merely the shadows of life on the wall of a cave, Panos. I've harbored few doubts in life, but in my advancing age some few have trespassed my mind's barriers, causing great unease."

"You have been one of life's true heroes, Amer," responded Panos, "committed to truth and integrity." Both men stood up and hugged each other before parting ways.

# XXXVI

Exiting the first-class club lounge where members could have a private shower while waiting for the next flight, Diana was a half-pace ahead of Kleïs, both dressed as two masculine airline pilots with black leather brief cases. Each seemed comfortable with life as they paced down the main departure hallway with erect postures, well-pressed suits, and confident smiles. Each was handsome with dark hair, smooth tanned skin, and crisp uniforms. They waved to the attendants checking in passengers queuing at various independent airline counters, quickly but carefully scrutinizing those in line.

Periodically a confident Diana would pause and converse briefly as both women observed the retinue of taxis discharging people on the way into the terminal. Then they proceeded back to the main hallway in front of the ticket counters. When one or two colleagues appeared to recognize them, they would give a brief salute, smiling at the others. A woman nearby, observing the elegant pilots, was heard to say that it is reassuring to see these men on the concourse looking so professional, what with all the bad news about flying and airline safety. One elderly woman stopped them and said confidently, "I know you two wouldn't invite young women to the cockpit during a commercial flight," referring to a much circulated photograph of a co-pilot of the missing Malaysian airplane bound for Beijing in 2014. Diana was pleased with the effects of their disguises.

A small stairway led to a first-floor loft above the ground floor where passengers and flight crews could sip coffee from a perch above the crowd, passing the time away with observations of travelling strangers below. The airline pilots walked up and found a table for two with a clear view of the crowd. Leaving caps and dark glasses on, each began to sip espresso slowly, scanning the anonymous sea of people preparing for departure.

"Diana, it's so confusing, so strange. You're my sister! How is it possible?" asked Kleïs. Rubbing her fingers at the inside corners of her eyes, Kleïs said, "What does that mean for us? What do we say to our fathers? I don't know, but I know that I love you. I'm just caught off guard."

"I don't know," said Diana, "but surely our fathers will have to fill us in with more detail. I am as stunned by the news as you are. We will get the answers. For now, my love, let's keep our eyes focused."

Diana motioned to Kleïs, "Look! What a happy family going on a trip!" Diana saw the carefree smiles of a slightly pudgy man, about 40 years old, an attractive wife and teenage daughter with flowing black hair. The gentleman wore tan slacks, a bright red tropical shirt, and a light blue sport coat. He was holding the tickets and pointing to a restaurant, full of booths and a small tapas bar. He nodded to his right, indicating that he would quickly meet them in the restaurant and walked towards *El Baño – hombres*.

---

Walking into the bathroom, the man in the tropical shirt could never have imagined the turbulence about to interrupt his flight to peace, Ramón thought. Eduardo appeared giddy about moving his family to Majorca, beginning a new life. Perhaps that pudgy shit imagined that with luck and reasonable probability, I would spend the rest of his life in prison after his capture by police. Fuck him!

Disguised as an elderly maintenance man with tan slacks and two orange stripes at the foot of each pant leg, Ramón had placed a sign "cerrado" – closed for cleaning – at the entrance to the rest room. He wore tinted glasses with dark frames.

In character as a maintenance man, despite a stiff walk and arms bent at the elbows, he walked softly as a cat behind Eduardo, who stood at the urinal, looking uncharacteristically youthful and energetic. He moved his hands on either side of Eduardo's face as though placing a spell on him, then quickly pulled the garrote back astride the man's neck.

Eduardo tried to grasp the restraint without success. Ramón whispered, "Sorry to be such a terrible pain in the neck, my friend. And so rude to interrupt you while voiding." Eduardo made a quiet barking sound as he tried to inhale, his eyes bulging with the obstructed flow of blood. Just as Eduardo was about to leave earth, Ramón loosened the garrote, spun him around and removed his spectacles so that his last vision would be the purple eyes of his assassin.

"Look at me, you little turd! No one can double-cross Ramón and live. Your wife and daughter will be next. Now think about that!"

Ramón completed the task, dragging the dead weight of the victim towards a huge trash bin. He took a minute to place Eduardo into a large brown plastic bag, then deposited the body inside. He hid the garrote in the toilet at the far end of the room, closed the door, and began to replace the earlier sign with one reading *out of order*.

Ramón was feeling pleased with himself. He would proceed quickly to the concourse where all bins were carted later to a platform. Subsequently the contents of the trash bins would be emptied into a large truck below for grinding and compression. Later he would ask some friends to trace the two-million euros that had been stolen from him by Eduardo. He was feeling confident and proud. Once he got his money back, this would all be a forgotten intermission in his life. Surely the police would discover that Eduardo was a psychopathic killer.

---

The two airline pilots left money on the table and scampered down the stairs towards the restroom. Kleïs asked Diana, "Are you prepared?"

"Yes," said Diana. "A designer product created just for this man, this vulnerable man," she said, pointing to a carnation covering one of her lapels.

Diana noticed the maintenance man leaving the bathroom and ushering a bucket on wheels and mop – away from the restroom, holding the "closed" sign in his right hand. He appeared anxious to get to this next job.

Something about the jovial man in the tropical shirt caught Diana's attention. Maybe it was how quickly it all happened after the man entered. Most cleaning people would wait until everyone had left the rest room before closing it off. There was something else - the maintenance man was so fit, despite his age, so strong in appearance. He seemed eager, enthusiastic to do his chores. And the trash can appeared to require effort, it was heavy with rubbish. Just then the rubbish man disappeared into a side door marked "For Authorized Personnel Only."

"Oh my god, Kleïs! It's Ramón, it's his build, his walk!"

# XXXVII

To security escorts in combat fatigues accompanied Jake and Chris, their wives, and four children out of their vehicles at the crowded airport. Supply trucks were traveling at high speeds, one officer remarked, making it a dangerous crossing for passengers anxious to get to the departure area. The police had just pulled over one man and were preparing to give the driver a ticket, remarking that the terror incidents were making people anxious and careless about entering and leaving the airport so quickly. The security officers halted traffic to allow a safe crossing and then led the way to the check-in location for British Airways. Everything went smoothly. The families were then led to airport screening clearance, where they quickly moved to the secure part of the airport and bade the officers thanks and farewell.

Still ill at ease, Jake reminded the children to stay together and not stray, not only because of recent threats but also because some schedules had changed as well as departure gates. Jake would not feel totally safe until lift-off.

He and Deb and the four children found adjoining seats facing the large windowpanes peering out on to the tarmac, while Chris and Mary looked for a snack to take on board. Sitting together away from the others, Jake and Deb said nothing and avoided eye contact.

Jake became more uncomfortable as the silence continued. Just above a whisper, he pleaded, "Deb, I am so sorry."

"Jake, you and I will need a holiday from each other when we return to Palo Alto."

For the first time in their marriage, Jake had no confidence that he could easily repair the emotional damage. Something else shook his consciousness: His marriage was important. His wife was important. The children were important.

"Deb, please don't make any rash decisions. We're both stressed out, and I plan to be a more attentive husband and father." He took two ibuprofen capsules from in his satchel and rotated his head back and forth looking for a water fountain.

"I don't think the family is important to you, Jake." Deb took a tissue from her pocket book to wipe her eyes. "You're selfish, and you don't care. To tell the truth, you've become less important to us." She paused for Jake to understand the significance of what she just said. "Get yourself a drink to drown out any small amount of guilt you may have. It may take you some time to recognize one of life's surprising truths, but the more you distance yourself from us, the less important you are. I've run out of patience. So belly up to the bar of your inflated importance."

Her voice was strident to Jake, whose hopes for some rapprochement were dashed by her resolution and pain. Jake started to speak, but Deb held her hands out like a policemen stopping traffic, "No!"

With that, she stood up, blotted a tear from her cheek and walked toward the children. She wanted to hug them, yearning for an earlier time in her marriage when both were toddlers, when life was carefree, love was complete and never in question.

First, she would regain her composure, walk up and back on the main hallway, frequently turning to keep her children in sight. I can't wait to be out of here, she thought. This whole fucking trip had been a disaster. She passed a man and woman in their 30s, examining each other's faces with intense desire, embracing and kissing as though they were alone in the world, no one else nearby to observe them. Good luck to you both, she thought. Grow together with each other and maintain your loyalty, trust, and love throughout your married life. It's hard work.

In the waiting area seats for a flight to Rome, two Italian children about 10 years old were having an animated conversation with their parents. Each had a yellow t-shirt with red short sleeves and the words *I ♥ Barcelona* in English written on the front. In her own mind she asked the children: Why – What do you love about this city? Do you have any idea of the pain and horror here? Do your parents have a clue to the city's dark side?

A young mother in her late twenties was rocking her infant to sleep as he lay in her arms. A proud father sat down next to her with two coffee containers. Both looked sleep-deprived but comfortable, as though completely pleased with the hand that life dealt them.

Checking her watch to see how much time was left before the flight, she realized that she had walked 15 gates from her own departure site, so lost in her thoughts had she become. A slight wave of guilt and anxiety rose in her neck, and she turned around abruptly. She needed to hug the children, though not to explain why this was so important.

In her intense focus to return to her departure gate, she hadn't noticed that an older man had been following her since her argument with Jake. He continued to push his rubbish container in front of him, aiming it directly in Deb's path. He bumped her softly with the container and quickly apologized in Spanish and English – "Lo ciento, sorry." He appeared lost, confused, yet polite and had a kind look about him.

Deb responded reflexively, "I'm so sorry."

The man appeared to limp, and he bent over as though injured in the mishap, pointed to his chest with a closed fist – a gesture all nurses have seen many times among victims of a heart attack. Deb inquired. "Are you all right, sir?"

She grasped his arm to offer help and he calmly whispered in English, "I have a gun in my hand and if you yell, I will shoot you and kill your children. Just come with me, and all will be right. I just need your help for a little while."

A wave of horror enveloped her. She felt light-headed and tremulous, fearful of fainting at that moment. Deb nodded to the man, telegraphing her compliance with his orders.

Her goal was to stay alive. She did not know who this man was, why he was kidnapping her, but she had to stay focused for herself and her children.

She had read enough about women in captivity to know it helped to keep the captor talking, to establish some form of a relationship, to appear understanding. "Who are you, and what do you want? I am a nurse and can help you, just let me know."

She could feel herself trembling. Her heart pounded forcefully in her chest as though sounding an alarm that an intruder had broken all the barriers, charging through the doorways to her mind. Glancing down the hallway, she saw no trace of Jake or security officers. Christ, where were they when you need them?

"Aqui, here," said the disguised Ramón.

He pointed to a side door. He punched in the security code for access. Then, leaving the trash bin outside in the hallway, both went inside.

Deb felt a sharp pain at the top of her head and lost all consciousness.

# XXXVIII

J oaquin Lopez, the aide to Spain's prime minister, was on hand to greet the delegates, arriving on Concourse B. Members of the press waited onsite at the request of authorities to show that the country was secure and not cowering in the face of cyber terror. Lopez counted fifteen newspaper reporters with support teams and five TV networks.

The foreign delegates and their staff filed in, surrounded by heavy security. They walked one-third of the way down the corridor, before exiting to a heavily guarded section of the entrance to the tarmac and into secure limousines waiting to transport them to the meeting venue. The entire concourse was closed to all but the delegation, security personnel, and screened members of the press.

Initially all questions from the media were directed at Lopez. What was the government doing to stop the terrorists? Was the health care system unraveling? Did he have clues to the names of the perpetrators and their goals? How many patients had died? Shouldn't the international meeting of foreign dignitaries have been cancelled in the face of terror? Could this be ETA, and if so, what was the evidence?

Lopez smiled through the tough questions and responded confidently in the understated lexicon of diplomats. "I am saddened, to say the least, that we have this problem," he said. "We're confident that it will be resolved soon. Law enforcement experts are following up on many leads. All precautions to safeguard the diplomats are in place, and we are also confident that the public's health will be maintained. There is no need to panic."

The prime ministers of the U.K. and France arrived about the same time at the airport and were converging in the middle of the concourse with their full delegations of about ten people each. The press crammed in closely to ask the British prime minister if he had concerns that his pacemaker would fail. He said he had this issue fully evaluated in preparation for the meeting and had no worries. "I am grateful for the opportunity to meet in Spain."

Similarly, France's prime minister said his diabetes had been well controlled, his insulin pump was working perfectly, and he had no concerns for his own health. He too emphasized the importance of the meeting in Spain and the propitious opportunity to effect some changes favorable for peace in the Middle East. "One cannot sit on the sidelines when a multinational alliance could result in an important change in the lives of so many," he said.

As the two descended the stairway to awaiting vans and more security personnel, two loud shots pierced the din of airport noise. Immediate panic followed. "Everybody down! Stay down!" yelled several security agents. Lopez drew a weapon, and swung it in the direction of the noise while people fell screaming to the ground. Through his earpiece, Lopez was informed that two large metal containers had dropped off a fork lift on the tarmac. All was well. People rose to their feet, still quite anxious, nerves frayed.

In turn the delegations from China, Russia, and the United States arrived and responded calmly to each of the questions posed before being escorted to the meeting. Each was asked about heart disorders and diabetes. Did they have any medical device in place? All indicated "no" and kept walking.

Many local passengers whose original flights had been posted for the Concourse B were confused. Lopez tried to steer clear of their questions but fielded many anyway. Several asked why they were being asked to move away. Where would the new gate be located? Was there a terror problem at the airport? The mood of travelers was also angry, though the police tried to assure them that they needed this area to prepare for foreign dignitaries. Nothing else was communicated. The sentiment among travelers was that the police were not telling them everything, some suggesting that the authorities were lying.

---

Elizabeth stood with Toni and Javier at the entrance to Concourse B. She scanned every person nearby but felt reasonably comfortable that the arrival of the foreign dignitaries and the departure of Chris and Jake and their families were both going smoothly. Once this part of the mission was completed, the trio would reconvene in town, collect any new intelligence on the whereabouts of Diana Kontos, and review updates on the investigation of the horrific murder of the owner of Tio Pépe's. Elizabeth received a few leads on Diana Kontos and her companion and relayed them to Toni and Javier. Some suggested that the two proprietors of Tio Pépe were linked to Diana. It wasn't clear how all this fit together.

From MI-5 and information from the secret intelligence service, MI-6, reports surfaced that Diana Kontos and a person known only as Kleïs were together at meetings of terrorists in Corsica. They were likely partners in crime, and the suspect called Kleïs was known to have computer hacking skills with links to hackers in the Eastern Europe and the Middle East. Elizabeth felt the connection between those two and Ramón was likely.

"So," said Elizabeth, "it is possible that something went wrong, and she may be behind the killing."

"Possible," said Toni, "but this looks like a hate crime, or a revenge or passion crime. In a bad partnership, I would expect a quick and unexpected death. Of course there could be a crime of passion."

"She indeed has such a history," said Elizabeth, recalling how Diana had paralyzed Ata Atuk, a double-crossing accomplice, jabbed him with botulism toxin and blinded him with injections of bacteria into his eye.

"No question that Pépe and Ramón are linked to the drug community," said Javier, "and this surely fits an assassination killing sending a strong warning from the underground."

"When money's at risk," said Toni, "Love is never lost in gang feuds. Even Pépe and Ramón could have argued with the banda's Jefe about money."

"In any case we need to get to the bottom of this," Toni said. "The clock continues to move on, and time kills deals and investigations. Our cyber team is restoring some of the computer functions at hospitals. We're asking all people with devices to have them reprogrammed. But even now the city remains terrorized. People are still running to banks before leaving for other towns with relatives."

Elizabeth yawned from real fatigue and acknowledged her sense of lassitude and ennui. "This is the part of law enforcement I like least. The waiting, no action, no pursuit, no interviews, just being sure people got on and off planes safely. Gentlemen, I can't wait to get on with our work when we return to town. I prefer action."

# XXXIX

W ith a nagging headache, Jake returned from the sports bar, his arms weighed down with four mugs of beer. He hoped the effects would reduce the tension between Deb and him. He glanced at the four children in friendly conversation sitting near Chris and Mary and offered the drinks to his friends. They gladly accepted.

"Where is Deb?" Jake asked. He repeated the question to his children, "Where is your Mom?"

Brice said he thought he saw her walking towards the ladies' room down the hallway. "It was just after you left."

Mary stood and said she would check. She would return quickly, she assured Jake, and handed her beer to Chris. "We women like to freshen up a little before a trip."

Chris and Jake moved a few steps away from the children. "Jake, everything else OK with you two?"

"Not at all, Chris," Jake answered with a little gravel in his voice. "Spending time with Elizabeth, helping with the epidemiological data, and then meeting Elizabeth again last night has taken a toll."

"It's likely that Deb wanted to be alone for a while or to punish you by frightening you. She and Mary may need a moment before they return. You know you deserve this, my friend."

Jake nodded in abject misery and embarrassment, looking down at the floor, not wanting eye contact with Chris. "I'm sick, Chris. I feel stupid."

A few minutes later Mary returned with a concerned look. "I looked in the nearest two ladies' rooms, Jake, one to the left and one way to the right of this gate and saw no sign of Deb." She sighed deeply. "I'm worried."

Jake softly confided to Mary that he and Deb had argued just before he left to get the beers, and she had walked off. "But with all the security concerns we have, it wouldn't be like her to disappear," he suggested. "Besides she was so worried about the children, even in this secure part of the airport. This is completely out of character," he reasoned.

"Jake, let's ask the airline to make a loudspeaker announcement," said Chris. "You know, ask her to return to her gate, that her family is worried and looking for her."

Mary said she would handle it and walked over to the service counter a few gates away. Within four minutes two repeated announcements came over the loudspeakers, "Would Deborah Evans on a flight to London please return to her flight's departure gate at once."

Five minutes later, with no sight of Deb, Jake realized that their flight's departure was only 45 minutes away. This made no sense. Why would she do this? Of course, she was angry with him, but she would never frighten the children.

Jake heard a horrible scream about 10 gates away. A woman was yelling repeatedly.

At first he thought it was Deb, but then the woman was speaking hysterically in rapid Spanish. Jake raced there, finding a flight agent trying to comfort a terrified traveler. She had thrown away some trash into a container, only to find a body inside. Within seconds, airport security men armed with AK-47 rifles ran to the scene from both directions.

The police had been on high alert for some time after a Spanish woman had reported her husband missing. The three family members had been scheduled to fly to Majorca, but he had disappeared after using the rest room. Disappeared without a trace. Security agents had inspected the rest room fully and found no one. They would have to identify the body in the trash bin.

Two security agents looked into the trash container. One said that the victim was a man wearing a colorful tropical shirt. The other agent grabbed the man's arm and felt for a pulse. He said to his partner that the man was dead. No pulse and no breathing, his face, totally without color. Several agents then pulled the man from the bin and placed him on the floor. In Spanish one said, "No question, he's a goner."

Jake got even closer and flagged down one of the agents. "Look, I certainly hope there is no connection, but I am Dr. Evans and my wife went missing forty-five minutes ago. I'm really worried."

What if the murderer had run into Deb? Maybe he was hiding in the ladies room when she went in.

Jake learned the agent's name was Alejandro del Rio. He and his colleague listened carefully to Jake's details and asked a lot of questions. "How long was she missing? Which direction did she walk? Was it unusual for her to do this before a flight? Was she on any drugs that might affect her thinking? Who else is traveling with them, and where are they?"

The agents' attentiveness accelerated when Jake responded to new questions. "What is your occupation? What was the purpose of your trip? Whom did you meet during his visit? Where did you stay?"

Agent del Rio said he would immediately alert his colleagues. He asked two female agents to check every rest room on the concourse at once.

Jake's breathing became heavy and accelerated. He pulled out his iPhone, turned away from the children, and dialed Elizabeth.

"Elizabeth, it's Jake. My wife is missing, and the body of a Spanish man has just been found on our concourse stuffed in a trash bin. Please help me."

"Jake, I am so sorry. I'll meet you there right away. Hopefully, your wife is safe somewhere close, but we'll look at all possibilities."

Jake relayed the message to Chris and Mary and gave a sanitized summary to the children. Word was rapidly spreading that a dead man was found in a large trash container, but none of that seemed important. "Where is Mom?" both children asked in unison. They were on their feet, clearly frightened. Jake sensed they seemed angry with him for allowing her to disappear.

———————

Only twenty meters away, Deb listened to her kidnapper. "I mean you no harm, Miss," said Ramón in a warm tone. "I have one question. I have seen your husband at the airport. I recognized him from a photograph; perhaps you have seen it. He was hugging a woman working for MI-5 in England. Obviously he is an unfaithful man despite his other accomplishments. So what I want to know, is this: is the MI-5 agent also here at the airport?"

"Yes, but I don't know where," said Deb. She sat on the floor; her hands were bound behind her with plastic ties. They were in a small room labeled *Private* off the hallway leading to the concourse.

"Here's what we're going to do. You will call your husband. Tell him that if he wants to see you again, he needs to instruct agent Foster to walk down Concourse C – by herself – unarmed, and with a cup of coffee in each hand. As soon as I see her, I will release you, Miss. Are we clear?"

"Yes, sir," said Deb.

She made the call. When Jake asked Deb how she was, Ramón ended the communication without a response.

Ramón placed ties on Deb's ankles and taped her mouth, hissing that if she made a sound or tried to move, he would kill her.

———————————

Jake relayed the message to Elizabeth. She told Jake to say, if contacted again, that they will follow all requests. "I'll arrive on Concourse C shortly. Don't get involved from here on, Jake. Don't even recognize me when I arrive, and keep both families in one area." She notified Javier and Toni, and all began to initiate a plan to safely recover Deb.

At 4 p.m., Elizabeth, in the center of Concourse C, walked slowly, systematically looking left and right and occasionally behind her. Though not changing her expression, she was furious that Jake had not followed her instructions. He was twenty meters behind her! But for his sake and hers, she continued. She held two paper cups with coffee, as instructed.

Travelers sat clustered in seats, leaving the hallway clear, as requested by first responders to the location of the dead man. A few airline and airport personnel passed by in both directions, as though no security problems existed.

Elizabeth approached the very end of the concourse and began a slow pacing back towards the beginning of the gate area. She neared a door marked *Private* when a maintenance man emerged, unnoticed by Elizabeth. Jake remained behind at the far end of the concourse.

Hearing the scuffing of feet, Elizabeth became startled and turned to see Ramón pace slowly behind her but on the side of the concourse, gradually shortening the difference to five paces. As he picked up his steps, Elizabeth noticed a pilot focused on an iPhone, and apparently not paying attention, brush his arm. The pilot apologized, turned, then proceeded briskly past Elizabeth. She wondered if the pilot had also sneezed on him, a slight mist seemed to have landed on his face.

Another man approached Ramón. He appeared to be an average traveler, barrel-chested and tall with features suggesting a Basque heritage.

Elizabeth was relieved to see Javier walk directly in front of Ramón, preparing to pull out a revolver from his pocket. Angry at the interruption, Ramón tried to take him down. He turned his body in a counter-clockwise motion, lifted his thigh, and released a savage roundhouse kick to the head of the intrusive traveler.

Javier blocked the kick with his left arm, taking such a blow that he wondered if the bones in his forearm had been broken. Despite the pain, he sank a powerful right-handed hook into Ramón's jaw, causing his head to snap back. Ramón remained standing.

Elizabeth could sense that Javier was shocked that the man was able to sustain consciousness after such a blow. She watched Javier prepare to follow up with a right cross. Yet as the two faced each other, Ramón clutched his throat and fell to the ground in a dead faint.

She could see Toni running from the near end of the concourse with his weapon in hand. Jake ran to Elizabeth's side despite her signal to stay away.

"What happened to him?" asked a quizzical Javier.

Jake ran to Elizabeth, where Ramón lay with swollen lips. He was wheezing and making barking sounds when he breathed in, as though there was some obstruction high in his airways.

"Elizabeth, there is some powder on the man's face. It has a terrible odor. I think he is having a severe allergic reaction to it, anaphylaxis. He'll die without epinephrine and antihistamines and may need critical care."

Elizabeth exclaimed, "She's here! Diana Kontos is somewhere near. Oh my God, the airline pilot who bumped into him!"

# XL

First responders arrived quickly to attend to Ramón, injected one, then a second dose of epinephrine. He would be transferred to a local hospital's emergency room. Intermittently, Ramón seemed to open his eyes briefly as though to get the attention of the medics, then close them slowly in some form of sleep. Fortunately for Ramón, the city hospital with excellent services was only minutes from the airport. Ramón was lifted onto a gurney by the medical team and led out of the airport by two policemen.

Elizabeth assured Jake that she would order a room-by-room search for Deb. The airport would be cordoned off from new arrivals. All people would be asked to stay in place until Deb could be found. Meanwhile, pictures of Diana Kontos were being emailed to all law enforcement people at the airport, stating that she was dangerous and considered armed.

Jake walked back to hug Tracy and Brice. "Where is Mom?" asked Tracy.

"I don't know, sweetheart, but the best detectives in the world are looking for her. I'm sure they'll find her safe. The authorities have told me that they think she is safe and not too far away."

Tracy looked at her Dad, unconvinced but trying to stay positive.

All outgoing flights were now put on undefined delays. The two families settled in for an anxious wait. Every fifteen minutes, Elizabeth called. The message was always the same. "We've not sighted her yet, Jake."

Four calls – and an hour went by for the anxious travelers.

Tracy was visibly shaken and crying. "Why weren't you with Mom, Dad?"

"I was, darling, until I left to get us a drink. When I returned she was gone. I'm so sorry, and I thought we would all be safe on this side of the security screening."

Feeling exhausted, Jake retraced all of the steps – missteps – leading to the discord between him and Deb. Until this trip he had cheated on Deb only once, and that was over a decade ago after a night of wine with an Italian microbiologist with whom he escaped from a boring after-dinner presentation. The Brunello was among the best of Tuscany's wine, and the night of fantasy a wonderfully exciting sexual experience.

Meeting Elizabeth two years ago rekindled a new fantasy, again an attractive professional woman whom chance has placed in his path. The two years apart had only heightened his anticipation of seeing her, being with her. And the time with her would be a memory he would revisit frequently, he thought.

All of this had a price and exposed his exposing his shortcomings as a husband and a role model for his children. Deb was the glue in the household, providing predictable order and dedication. She was wonderful. And the children were a special joy, adding meaning to life's narrative, unconditional love and excitement. Now he might lose the three most important people in his life, and it would not have been worth the brief pleasures with another woman. What the fuck was wrong with him?

He vowed to be a new person if the family came out of this ordeal unscathed. He would beg Deb to forgive him. He resolved at that moment to see a psychiatrist when he returned to Stanford; he needed to understand why he risked so much of what he loved, what he needed. He was comfortable with the idea of therapy. He would do anything to get his family back.

After ninety minutes, Jake's phone went off. "We've found her, Jake. She's OK but has had an injury. Stay where you are, and I'll bring her to you."

"Thank God!" said Mary, hearing the news. Chris too seemed elated, and Jane came over to Brice to give him a hug. Jake hugged both his children.

Elizabeth, flanked by Toni and Javier, appeared down the corridor, pushing Deb, who was sitting in a wheelchair. She had a large bruise on her right cheek. That side of her face was swollen, but she was alert and speaking coherently.

Jake and Deb hugged. In Elizabeth's eyes, Jake looked completely unglued. As two physicians from the airport arrived to examine Deb, Elizabeth signaled Jake to come with her.

"Jake, your wife has been knocked unconscious – you know better than I what that may imply clinically. We found her tied up and gagged and bruised. Her description matched that of a man named Ramón, an underworld figure tied to narcotics and possibly to Diana Kontos. It was his business partner who was found brutally murdered. If your wife is stable, take her from here on the next flight to London and get away from this world of mine and all of its dangers. I'll ask my colleagues to assign police protection until you all board the plane.

"You have been instrumental in helping us see the problem, but it has cost you, and I'm sorry. I will always be grateful for your help.

"She asked if I was the other woman. I told her that I was, but that the affair is over." Looking directly at Jake, she said: "I apologized to your wife, Jake, and I hope it helps a little.

"You are going to have to work hard to repair your marriage, and I apologize to you also for my contribution to that problem." She briefly paused to collect her thoughts. "My life and my happiness are linked to my marriage, my husband and family. I know that now. It's clear."

Recognizing both the finality of Elizabeth's words and their truth, Jake still felt a sense of rejection. He wished he didn't, but it was there and it was uncomfortable. He felt sad.

In an extraordinarily brief period of time, Jake imagined a pleading oath to Deb. He would care for her injury first, pay constant attention to her emotional needs while repeatedly apologizing. He would reorganize his time at the hospital, spend more time at home, and arrange for weekend events with both children and Deb. He was cautiously hopeful, a new man in the making after a crisis of large proportion.

"Goodbye, my friend," said Elizabeth. She turned and walked away.

# XLI

Throughout the airport, Diana noticed security agents checking everyone's identification and forcing crowds of people on all concourses to stand in long lines. Word was circulating that several incidents at the airport had caused the two- to three-hour departure delays. Diana overheard travelers saying that the police were looking for someone or several people. Why else would they be checking ID information? And she told Diana about the rumors of a dead man found in a large rubbish bin had everyone on edge. Who was he anyway? Was all this related to the cyber terror incidents at hospitals and clinics? Who was the lady found unconscious in a room off the main concourse? In her pilot's uniform, Diana simply replied, "No one knows yet."

Walking down one of the long corridors between major concourses, it was obvious to Diana that the din of the crowd pondering those questions made all but the loudest and most articulate of public announcements over the loudspeaker completely unintelligible.

She and Kleïs found themselves surrounded by security agents. They had impeccable identification documents and were stopped only briefly.

Noting a small amount of yellowish white powder on Diana's lapel, one security agent, a 50-year-old woman, asked permission to brush it off. Commenting on how attractive they were, she politely asked if she could pose with them for a selfie on her iPhone. The pilots consented, although with some apparent reluctance.

Observing the frown on Kleïs' face, Diana responded, "I know we shouldn't have done that, but we also don't want to create a scene. We don't want any delays."

Kleïs nodded. Both were pleased that they had neutralized and likely eliminated Ramón, exposing him to an aerosol of sulfa, to which he was exquisitely allergic of course. It would take more time to find the money he stole.

---

Toni and Javier sent out a broadcast email to stop all airline pilots from leaving the active concourses for international flights. Specifically, it specified all pilots be held until Toni, Javier, or MI-5 agent Elizabeth Foster could question each.

Toni received an email from a woman at her security post, with the selfie attached, asking if these were people of interest. She explained that it was taken only minutes before the mandate to stop pilots.

---

Diana and Kleïs were now in the general hallway of the airport, but to their dismay found that all exits were cordoned off. The number of police reinforcements was swelling. They needed to create the diversion both had planned on. Time for Kleïs to bring out her cell phone.

Within seconds all the electricity was off in the airport. Lights went out. The jet ways came to a halt, and the moving sidewalk was frozen. The computers used to check the validity of international travelers were stalled, beltways were now motionless with luggage. All screening technology stopped working and air-conditioning ended.

Alarms went off, people screamed in panic. Some cell phones were dysfunctional as people tried to contact friends and family members or search social media.

Kleïs sighted one of the expensive boutique shops for women nearby and signaled to Diana that they should enter.

"We're shopping for our wives and saw these beautiful ladies' suits. We'd like one for each of us to take home. Fortunately, we have cash, so no need to wait for a functioning cash register." Looking around, Kleïs added, "Those are beautiful hijabs. We'll also take one each."

The clerk was pleased to make the sale of two fashionable, two-piece black suits and presented each pilot with a package and carrying bag.

The two pilots thanked her profusely. They removed their caps and jackets, brushed their hair quickly and walked to the ladies' rooms. Two stalls stood open. Each changed into new outfits. They stuffed the pilots' uniforms in the exclusive store bags and deposited them into large rubbish bags on the way out. The two ladies walked arm in arm towards the exit, like somewhat liberated women from Morocco.

Toni confirmed that the photo showed Diana Kontos with an unidentified person, both dressed as male airline pilots. She asked Javier and Toni to redouble their efforts in closing the airport to all people. They needed to establish an area where everyone could be observed and special attention given to questioning all airline pilots.

Diana and Kleïs in tailored suits and headscarves looked for any weaknesses, any lapse of the airport security perimeter. Even the large number of police could not help being overwhelmed by the huge crowds coming and going.

Seizing an opportunity, Diana and Kleïs swiftly passed through the blind spot of the screening area. They were unaware that someone noticed that they had not been screened.

Suddenly a man's voice behind them yelled in Spanish, "Stop those women! Stop them!" Turning around they saw a giant of a man racing towards them with huge strides. He was closing the gap, now twenty-five meters away.

A few Muslim men stood in Toni's way. They demanded, "Why are you chasing two of our sisters? Stop, Señor."

Toni pushed them aside easily, continuing to call out "Halt! Halt!" The women made it out of the airport's entrance. Elizabeth and Javier followed.

A getaway car waited 100 meters away, perfectly positioned to lead to a major highway. Diana and Kleïs were breathless racing across the first of three two-lane roads separated by walkways for passengers awaiting pick-ups from friends or family, public taxis, buses to downtown, and courtesy lanes for nearby hotels.

The women dodged anxious drivers, who sped out after picking up passengers. Horns blared as Diana and Kleïs made it to the second road, after nearly being hit by a city bus. Toni was closing in.

The Porsche with keys in place was now only one crossing away. All they needed to do was get in and race to freedom.

The women ran across the third lane of traffic, continually looking back at Toni. He yelled, "Cuidado! Be careful! Halt!" Both turned to see how close he was and failed to see an oncoming truck. Diana reached back, grasping Kleïs' hand, hoping to pull her to safety.

---

Toni heard screeching brakes and a thumping crash that left both women lying motionless on the street. He stood above the two fugitives and waited for the paramedics, followed shortly afterwards by Javier and Elizabeth.

The paramedic attending Kleïs placed a collar around her neck to stabilize the spine and made sure to position her for an open airway. She moaned continually but was breathing, even if very slowly. He opened her eyes and noted that one pupil was much larger than the other. "Probably a brain bleed," he blurted out to his colleague.

The second paramedic took vital signs on Diana, opened her airway and moved quickly to splint both lower legs, which appeared to have sustained compound fractures. Diana said nothing. The paramedic called out, "Give her some room" to people walking by and gawking.

In five minutes two ambulances arrived to take the women to an emergency room.

"What are their chances?" asked Toni.

"Marginal," responded one of the paramedics.

Looking at Diana, and then back to Javier, Elizabeth said, "It's been a long time, but the world is safer now. I do regret our inability now to question her and her associate, to try to understand the minds of such dedicated terrorists. If they survive, we may gain special insights not only to motives but also to malware sophistication."

Javier confirmed earlier reports that the accomplice was also a Greek woman with ties to a terrorist group in Corsica, skilled in cyber terror. She apparently had a few colleagues programming malware in Malta,

Russia, and Palestine. "Now the lights will go on and Spain will breathe a little easier!"

Javier also recognized that fear and uncertainty persist after a terror event, despite its resolution. Public confidence in the government was damaged , and other groups may surface in the meantime to divide the citizens, even threatening to secede. Where that would go was unclear.

# XLII

The trio of agents met again in the small conference room near Toni's and Javier's offices. The exhaustion was palpable. So was the relief.

Javier began. "Just heard, Elizabeth, from the hospital where Ramón was being treated. He's fighting for his life on a respirator."

"I hope he makes it," said Elizabeth. "Although many criminals define banality, I would try to see his motives, understand his relationship to Diana and the Corsican terror group. I'll leave early tomorrow on a flight back to London," she added. "I'm looking forward to seeing my children, my husband, and colleagues at MI 5. The end of Diana Kontos closes a personal quest for me. I believe this will restore some lost confidence in me after I let her escape two years ago in London."

"I'm glad. It's been a pleasure working with you," said Javier, "We will keep in contact, let you know how Diana's condition is. Your relationship with the two doctors was critical to our response time. We can now allow our government to work in earnest to solve critical international issues without having to think about the welfare of visiting dignitaries."

"Agreed," said Toni, reaching out to high-five the other two. "It's time for you to go home, too, Javier. I'll stay to wrap up the details with my assistant who has agreed to help me with a final or near final report."

"Thanks, Toni, and goodbye, Elizabeth," said Javier. They all shook hands.

Toni returned to his desk and began to dictate a report for his assistant. Twenty minutes later she announced that an elderly man had called with information on the women cyber terrorists and had just arrived. "I left him downstairs in the lobby. Should I tell him to call for an appointment tomorrow?"

"Sure. Wait, no. I guess I can see him now in the small conference room. I'm curious what he may know. Give me three minutes to complete a paragraph or two, then you go home soon! I can finish early tomorrow."

"Yes, sir, thank you. I'll be on my way in a few minutes and will see you tomorrow." She escorted the visitor to the conference room.

Toni walked into the conference room to greet the elderly man and extended his arm to shake hands. The man seemed even older to Toni than his secretary had described, perhaps, as a result of a sadness that appeared to cover his scarred face combined with the pallor of someone who is ill.

"I'm a businessman from Crete. I have been following closely the cyber-ware attacks that have paralyzed this beautiful city. I think I have insights into the people involved that may be of interest." He paused briefly to catch his breath.

"I travel frequently and have many international colleagues, some of whom may be thought to be unsavory. I usually don't pay attention to that so long as my business does well. But sometimes these connections give me insights that I would never have otherwise appreciated. I thought it worthwhile to pass these on to you, sir.

"On television today I saw the faces of two women implicated in the cyber terror, appearing to be young male airline pilots, then with an airport security woman, and then another image of both on the street, having been severely injured by a truck. They were so vital in one photograph and then lifeless in another, only minutes apart. Makes you reflect on the absurdity of life. I heard that their chances of survival are very low.

"I thought I recognized one of them, and I can tell you what I know to be true. I was shocked to see her alone with her close friend lying still on the road to the airport. Some people just walked by her unconcerned, making no attempt to help."

Seeing the man's expression and hearing a slight harshness in his voice, Toni rose to get a glass from the far side of the table. He filled it with water from a fountain in the hallway and brought it to his visitor.

"Thank you again, sir. This will help me." He took a swallow of water.

"You see she was always the life of the party," said the visitor, "With friends all over the world. I am told she was gifted in computers, committed to help the downtrodden wherever they lived. I can gladly give you her home city and a list of people with whom she worked."

"That would be extremely helpful, sir, for continuing our investigation," responded Toni, his interest quite piqued.

"No problem, commander." The guest paused to get his breath again and to sip some water. "My voice is abandoning me, I fear. Sorry for the interruption."

Toni waved his hand to imply that he needn't apologize.

"From everything I know, Commander, she was always a caring individual who saw the unjust in life and committed herself to various causes to repair inequities. Perhaps, along the way, she received some poor advice or was somehow cajoled into an occasional bad or unwise cause. She was so passionate about helping people that she could easily have been misled, making mistakes of the head, never of the heart." The old man clasped his left hand over his own chest, looking sad.

"I'm grieved to tell you, sir, that I know her father well. He will surely be devastated and may not recover from this. He too has been a dedicated servant to the poor and vulnerable people globally. In a very real way, she has two fathers, two men in the late stages of life that will grieve until their last days. The bond between the two men and their daughters was extraordinary powerful.

"Are you a religious man?" inquired the visitor. "I mean do you believe in heaven and hell?"

Toni thought the question odd, out of place from a stranger. He brushed off the question as unimportant but acknowledged that as a Catholic he hoped for some life after death. He refocused on the elderly man.

Toni's assistant came by to say goodbye and mention that MI-5 agent Foster had another question and would be by soon. But she decided not to interrupt him and she left the building.

"So how exactly do you know this lady and her father, may I ask?" inquired Toni. "And did you know her companion as well?"

The man reached into his pocket to pull out a cell phone as though to query it for some information. He held up a photograph of Kleïs and himself smiling on a bright spring day on a hill overlooking Heraklion, the capital of Crete. "She loved Homer, Plato, and the old and new poets from Sappho to Cavafy. She was a student of Greek history and could recite many of the pages describing the Trojan War as told in the *Iliad*. And when she recited Sappho or Cavafy, you would be mesmerized. Describing life, she would often say that *Ithaca gave you the beautiful journey.*

"You see, sir, one of the women who ran from you today and may be dying was my beautiful daughter, my little girl whom you probably killed. The other was her partner in business and in life, another victim of yours."

An ominous shiver swept over Toni. He heard his own words of warning clamoring in his brain like a rogue wave smashing on the rocks, *Never let your guard down, especially when things look calm.* He stood up quickly, towering over his visitor just as Panos detonated the small plastic bomb strapped to his waist, triggering a blinding white flash.

———————————

Elizabeth raced towards the conference room from the end of the hall after she heard the thunderous explosion, which blasted the glass windows into shards showering over the city of Barcelona below, instantly ending the lives of the two men in conference.

# XLIII

At the hospital's emergency room, Ramón had initially been quickly triaged to a private room where vital signs were taken, IV fluids started, and another dose of epinephrine and of antihistamines were administered. "Good afternoon. I am Dr. José Morales. What's your name?" asked the doctor, looking over the clip board with all the clinical laboratory information. Briefly opening his eyes, Ramón whispered harshly, "Ramón."

"Well Ramón, you have lots of policemen here interested in you. But my only goal is to help you. Do you understand?"

Ramón nodded. He coughed twice, sounding like a dog's bark.

"You are very sick, Señor. You have a severe allergy response. Do you know what you are allergic to?"

"Sulfa," whispered Ramón. He strained to open his eyes. "Someone tried to kill me."

"We are giving you all the medications we know to treat this, Señor. But your blood pressure is low and you have some swelling deep in your throat. That is why you have trouble speaking and your cough sounded strange. We may need to give you drugs for your low blood pressure and likely put a tube down your wind pipe to hook you up to a breathing machine." He paused.

"As a matter of protocol, I need to ask, do you want us to do everything possible if your heart stops, including chest compressions?

"Si."

"Do you have any family or friends to call?"

Ramón looked up at the doctor. "Do you know where Diana is?"

"I don't know who that is Ramón, but we can look for her. What should I say to Señora Diana?"

His voice mumbling and soft, Ramón said "Tell her to fuck herself!" He then closed his eyes.

Morales called for the intubation kit and soon thereafter Ramón's breathing was controlled with a respirator. He was then called to another part of the Emergency Department to lead a resuscitation effort for a cardiac arrest patient. A bus accident near the airport caused minor injury to 10 patients, most of whom were arriving at the ED. All personnel were called to assist. Two policemen waited outside of Ramón's room.

Thirty minutes later, Morales returned to check on Ramón.

There was a low-pitched sound from the respirator, unlike the usual piercing note of ventilation failure. Looking at the recordings, Morales was shocked to see that the respirator had failed to support Ramón's breathing for fifteen minutes! This had never happened before. His patient was dead. He covered both eyes with his hands.

He notified the hospital's CEO, the two policemen, and the chief medical officer. He learned that two other respirators failed in the medical ICU, but vigilant nurses saw it and bagged the patients themselves until new machines could be delivered.

The chief medical officer suspected that the computer systems had been hacked and malware installed. This was no consolation to Morales, whose shift was ending.

He called home to his wife. "Queta, I'm on my way after the worst day of my career. Open up the Rioja and let me tell you what happened. I may leave emergency medicine. I may leave all of medicine."

As he put his phone down, Morales received a stat page to the emergency room. Two young women with severe traumatic injuries just arrived from the airport. "They are in critical condition and both required intubation. Outlook grave."

Morales would delay his planned early return home.

---

Next Morning

"Jake, Elizabeth here. I'm in the airport in Barcelona, awaiting my flight to London. Are you free to speak now?"

"I am, Elizabeth. I'm walking around Oxford trying to get my thoughts together. I'm surprised to hear from you."

"Jake, yesterday was the best and worst of my career. I saw the capture of Diana Kontos and her terrorist colleague, Kleïs, at last. But I've been awake all night, periodically trembling. I left but came back to Toni's office yesterday with a question for my report to MI-5. As I entered the hallway, a huge explosion coming from the conference room rocked the building. Toni and the man with him, thought to be Kleïs's father, were killed instantly.

"The sight was horrible! Body parts, glass shards, blood, and one wall completely blown out."

"Oh, my God! I'm so sorry. Are you OK?

"Yes. A few scratches only. But I'm still reeling from the shock of Toni's death and how close I came to being killed myself. My question is, can we stay in touch? I need to know how you feel."

"I'm more than confused, Elizabeth. One day you call it all off abruptly, and now you have a 180-degree change."

"I know, Jake. I'm sorry, but I think we can be close again if you want me."

"Elizabeth, my wife and I have had two intense discussions since we arrived in England. If I keep focused on my family, we can get back. I know she'll forgive me. She hasn't said so exactly, but I know her well, and I want to preserve what we once had. And I want my kids to love me.

"You said you wanted to return to your husband and that I needed my family. You were right."

"I understand Jake, and respect your thoughts. Once again, I cannot thank you enough for your expertise with the investigation. It was critical to our success. I don't expect our paths to cross again, so as I hang up, I sincerely wish you well."

# POSTSCRIPT

Dear Jake,

It's been two months since we've spoken. I know from discussions with the children that you are well and busy with work at Stanford. I've also learned that you decided to turn down the chair at Chicago, and I suspect that it relates to your desire to be close to our children. That took a great deal of thought and courage on your part. It would have been a wonderful career move. You deserve all the professional recognition you have received, and surely even more accolades will come your way in the future. I'm genuinely sorry that you had to make that choice.

Brice and Tracy continue to do well in school. You may know that Brice receives daily emails from Jane. It seems as though the European trip was an introduction to a special romance, even if an ocean away. The two lovebirds even Skype regularly. I'm not sure how it will work out, but I know Brice is already planning to have Jane fly over for his senior prom next year. In the meantime Jane and her family are planning a trip to

Tuscany to celebrate Jane's birthday in the spring. They've invited Brice to join them. I hope you'll pay for his flight.

Things are going well for Tracy, who has a few boys calling regularly. She has been on occasional dates to movies and bowling with friends. There doesn't appear to be anything serious developing, however.

My apartment is nice and surely adequate for the three of us.

My work is uneventful, which is okay for now. The OR seems to be in a stable period with few academic rivalries threatening its smooth function. The surgical services and wards are without major challenges.

I've missed you. The time apart has been difficult. When the kids are away with their various sports and activities, I miss having you around. I hate eating alone at night by myself.

You're also a wonderful dad. I was remembering the time you built a very special table from expensive English cherry wood. It took you months to cut and smooth and finish what became a beautiful piece of art, the highlight of our living room. We were all nervous we might harm it permanently with a wet glass. So much so that we avoided touching it. I remember when we gathered around it reverently, while you intentionally spilled red wine from your glass, letting it sit and saying, "Let's enjoy this!"

With all my alone time, I've also thought about us and the many good times we shared in our marriage. At our fifth wedding anniversary you arranged such a wonderful surprise visit to Napa at the most beautiful inn I could imagine. Flowers and champagne on ice awaited us in the room. I remember the magnificent French dinner and the lovely music you arranged. The evening was full of love and romance. Once again, you swept me off my feet.

My close friends remind me regularly what a good husband you have been, that all men are tempted to stray at some times, and that many do so. They say I would be foolish not to get back with you, that you surely love me, and that we could be a happy couple once again. I play those conversations over in my mind almost every night as I stare at the ceiling unable to sleep, often with tears running down my cheeks.

But in the light of day I view your cheating on me on two occasions as a huge betrayal. I cannot trust you anymore.

There is a gaping hole in my life, an emptiness that I cannot fill with good memories alone. It cries out for unwavering commitment and sacrifice. Nor can hope or promises or good intentions satisfy this hollowness. I am left with an emotional hunger that our marriage once satisfied. Now I find a marriage that has eroded and left me in a sunken place that I don't want or like.

In case you are wondering, there is no one else in my life, only you. But that is not enough. We've both discussed the beauty of life in earlier discussions, having witnessed its too early closure in too many of our patients. I seek pleasure, not the mere absence of pain. I want fulfillment, growth, humor, a sense of value, security, excitement. In a word, I seek identity. Somewhere along the line I've lost that. I love truth and beauty. And the sad truth is, I don't love you anymore. The only beauty out of this mess is that with truth, I have found myself once again.

I'm walking away from you and have shared with the children my recent filing for divorce. No need to call or write or email or send notes with the children. You know me well enough to understand this is a final decision.

Goodbye.

Deb

# ABOUT THE AUTHOR

Richard Wenzel is a physician and former chairman of the Department of Internal medicine at the Medical College of Virginia (VCU) in Richmond, Virginia, and like his character, Jake Evans, is an international authority on infectious diseases. He draws on his medical knowledge and worldwide experience to tell a story that takes us into the ailing heart of today's political and social realities. This is his second novel.